Brave Survivors are Superhumans

STEVEN ASOVSKY

Survivors are destined to save lives.
The brave never quit.

 FriesenPress

One Printers Way
Altona, MB R0G 0B0
Canada

www.friesenpress.com

Disclaimer: *Brave Survivors are Superhumans* is a work of dystopian fiction. Names, characters, businesses, organizations, places, events and incidents are the product of the author's imagination or are used fictitiously. Any resemblance to current events, locales or to living persons is entirely coincidental.

ISBN
978-1-03-916807-7 (Hardcover)
978-1-03-916806-0 (Paperback)
978-1-03-916808-4 (eBook)

1. FICTION, DYSTOPIAN

Distributed to the trade by The Ingram Book Company

Table of Contents

The Moon Eclipse. 1

The Curse of Notre Dame. 11

The Destruction of Nagasaki. 19

The Criminal and The Lion 35

Surviving Unimagined Dystopias 47

The Atlantic Ocean Meteorite: The Big Angel 57

A Family Vacation in Terror 63

The Farm 73

The Haunted House at Smithson Lane 83

The Dragon's Castle of Nottingham 95

A Convicted Serial Killer 117

The Mars Expedition 127

Las Vegas in Sandy Valley 135

Inside Planet Earth's Secret World. 143

Lost Island 151

The Natural Disaster of April 7, 2042 165

Chapter 1

The Moon Eclipse

On July 3, 2030, Kevin is in his steamy bedroom at 6:30 am and opens the window, sweats from the extreme heat. Smoggy air blows at his face—dizzy, falls over a chair onto the floor in excruciating pain. Later, regains consciousness, choking.

Kevin does not eat breakfast and goes out for a stroll under high radiation. He sees behind the rain clouds the infrared sun, which looks as if a heat event is in forecast. The bright sun accumulates humid conditions, making it difficult for him to predict precipitation.

Kevin rushes to the cooling centre to have chilled refreshments and to listen to the local news. People wait in the line to buy soft drinks; Kevin approaches the cash register with five American dollars in his back pocket.

He orders a refreshing drink for himself. "I want Diet Coke."

The cashier responds, "Three dollars, please."

After checking out, Kevin opens the front doors—sport fans watch a soccer game on television and he joins them until a seat is available. Young teens play their Nintendo games and they take the seats. He has to stand. Many people stand watching with excitement. Later, Kevin finds a spot and runs towards a sofa, a brilliant spot to cool-off, orders more soft drinks.

Kevin sits on the couch enjoying every moment of privacy, drinking his Diet Coke. Waiting for sunshine and cooler air, a brilliant spot to beat the heat. Out the window, an empty street with no crowds. It turns dark when strong winds blow gravel from different intersections, creating a big mess. The broadcast announces the moon eclipse will happen this evening. Many reacted. Kevin stays inside, devouring a tasty hamburger. Stomach ached from laziness.

Kevin reflects on his personal thoughts of the moon eclipse. This evening, no place to hide. Confused whether to escape fears or face the dangers alone. Spending long hours inside the cooling centre, the weather outside looks normal, but still a slight chance of seeing possible stormy conditions.

Through the window, a flashing white beam of light strikes the street, and buildings shatter from such of a dramatic force—dangerous as a 6.0 magnitude earthquake. Kevin and the others run outside, and the gibbous moon faces the apartment buildings. Damaged sidewalks make it difficult for everyone to walk on rubble. Public transportation is not in service and taxicabs trapped inside deep potholes. The greatest impact since the aftermath of Port-au-Prince's earthquake.

People stand in the parking lot hearing ambulance sirens. Heavy smoke pollutes the skies. Kevin runs on the road looking in both directions, witnessing the terrors of families rampaging in tears after watching their loved ones die. Kevin's apartment burns into toxic fumes. Trouble breathing on the spot, he cries in despair, having no money in his burned clothes.

Painful to see lost lives, destroyed cars towed from the garage by small trucks, and the fire department spraying water to stop the flames. Kevin walks towards a playground, a magnificent spot to plan his next steps, and finds other ways to protect himself before going to unusual places. Wanders in the empty playground where burned trees are at every corner within the ruins of dry soil as fires spread.

It is evening, the red sunset fades where radiant stars glitter the night skies, and the moonlight sheds darkness. What might happen if the moon eclipse replaces sunlight? Imagine.

The full moon glows brighter than the heavenly stars; a strange world is upon us. Natural evolution acknowledges the modern science of Earth's long history. This evening, the most thrilling spectacle, the moon eclipse *twice as large*, makes the night spooky when dogs howl in the moonlight. Destruction brings no electricity. Kevin has a terrible impression the moon will control Planet Earth, and climate change will form dangerous storms.

Past midnight, hearing the pain and suffering of injured people on the verge of their death. How sad to be living within a dystopian world where nature traumatizes people's minds. Kevin finds himself entrenched, having no sleep and not much to eat. Cannot figure out where will he head next.

Kevin wakes up beside a recycling bin at sunrise and runs to the street, and the sidewalk shakes from trucks going on damaged roads. He had this crazy idea to steal a truck and drive, live on his own, and overcome terrible experiences.

He follows the path towards an abandoned construction site where a truck is parked next to a crane, and jogs less than a half-mile from the park; the truck's door is wide open and the engine running. Speed-driving to the nearest highway, Kevin sees firetrucks battle the flames in every apartment building. Devastation is worse.

Kevin routes somewhere to isolate himself from the moon eclipse, risking his life while driving on a deserted highway, afraid of torrential rainstorms. Will he find a shelter in a hideout from mass destruction? Ready to make moral decisions?

Still riding along the path surrounded by massive spruce trees, no sign of a town or motel, Kevin does not know which road he's headed on. No cars on the roadway. A weird feeling of someone following, avoids risking pulling over for a nap. Kevin spots a town that looks safe for a stopover, to search for food. How many miles driven? Seeing the streetlights ahead; speed-driving on low fuel; a block away from arriving, the truck stops and smoke comes from the engine.

Walking a few metres towards the coffee shop—inside, a gang of bikers dressed as tough guys. Strolls, glancing through the dining section, paying no attention to anyone. Finds a seat somewhere quiet, away from strangers. At the dinner table, reading through the food menu, Kevin is hungry.

A server approaches. "May I take your order, sir?"

Kevin orders, "I want a bowl of clam chowder soup, fresh fries with ketchup on the side, and a strong coffee, including a Boston cream donut for dessert."

After a full hour of waiting, the server brings Kevin his delicious meal. Finishes eating, stays up late to make plans. If the moon eclipse appears at any moment, this is serious trouble for Kevin. Is saving his life from death more important than risking?

Leaves the restaurant with a full stomach, walks towards the motel on the other side of the street, and opens the entrance doors. A hotel manager named Brandon—a young, handsome, bold-looking man dressed as a business owner.

Kevin requests, "I want a small room for a few days, please."

"Sure. Do you have a credit card or cash?" Brandon replies.

Kevin responds, "I have twenty dollars in my pocket and I lost most of the money back home. Have you heard on the news about the moon eclipse disaster in LA?"

Brandon answers, "Yes. Not having enough money is the reason you're here?"

An explanation. "I have no place to stay. You see my dirty clothes. I didn't take a shower for days with no drinking water. May I please have the room for a few days and I will repay you for whatever sum you charge me?"

Brandon thinks. "Ok. Fine. Work for me with no wage until you reach two hundred dollars, which I will charge you. Do we have a pact?"

"Yes," Kevin agrees.

Unlocks the room. Kevin takes a warm bath after the rough day. Refreshed before sleep, for fifteen minutes he stands out on the balcony breathing the fresh air and listens to cricket sounds, watches the cloudy night skies, seeing no stars. In his hotel suite, fast asleep. The next morning, Kevin walks to the same restaurant, having a quick breakfast to eat something before his first workday. Assigned a temporary work position to be "concierge"—greet customers by giving their keys in old-fashion service. Brandon said the job is voluntary.

Nothing to wear, no coupons for dining, and no spare clothes. Besides this, Kevin in his adulthood life has never worked hard for nothing, a waste of time to handle tough duties while working for free! The key challenge he faces is completing the number of office hours assigned by Brandon, which could take more than a few workdays to reach the $200 target. Needs an extra workday to complete the tasks.

Brandon speaks, "You worked enough. I will let you stay here for two nights."

"Thank you," Kevin responds.

After this talk, Kevin feels tempted to have a smoke and a beer. A pleasant evening to enjoy the quiet moments before leaving tomorrow. Make something special? A small table of the food saved from yesterday's restaurant meal. Outside, a good snapshot of the gorgeous sunset, and the fraction-moon turns blue as shining stars create a living sky and a meteorite passes over!

Kevin sits on the balcony as the sky darkens. The moon is bloody-red, its translucent colour changing after a hot summer day. Next door, the others come out to check out the real moon eclipse and take amazing live photos with their cameras. It is midnight. The half-moon turns orange; the stars fade as it becomes cloudy after the moonlight's glowing beam.

A half-hour passes, the moon eclipse ends, nothing else to do but watch late-night television. Waking up the next morning at 9:00 am, Kevin opens the curtains, and it's freezing outside—early winter in the middle of July! Strange? Kevin goes back to his room, takes a warm shower, and packs for check-out from Brandon's hotel by 12:00 pm. Ready, Kevin closes the door behind him and goes for lunch. Along the stairwell, he sees Brandon lying on the floor unconscious. Runs to him fast, staring at his pale face and his weak body movement.

Brandon's words of his last breath:

"My hotel is yours. Swear to keep this place clean and in order by not forgetting my financial back account statements and bookkeeping."

Kevin calls the ambulance many times, and the phone line is dead. Runs outside looking for anyone who could help take Brandon to the hospital. Many fled from yesterday's moon eclipse. A strange yellowish-white sky with dust particles forms low cloud cover in the wake of an apocalyptic snowstorm.

Around, Kevin notices no vehicles. No clues how to bring Brandon to a nearby hospital—asking himself, should I carry him on my back as a brave soldier or leave him?

Kevin walks along the highway, Brandon's arms on shoulders. Mother Nature will not guide us through dangerous places. Observance is important. Fears will not stop Kevin from protecting Brandon.

Walks for over ten miles, having constant back pain, Kevin's sweat drips on the road. It is up to him to search for medicinal foods along the route and discover a place to sleep. Remaining cautious to avoid danger and deciding which place is better at hiding. It could take weeks or a month. Kevin is impatient when helping Brandon with no resources and mad about nobody coming to our rescue.

Kevin witnesses humanity in catastrophe, fighting for Brandon's life. Keeping a close eye on danger, no rain for the past couple of weeks and parched weather. They have nothing to feed themselves. Everywhere is dry and no trees.

Looking at the skies, the full moon comes out and blankets Earth, covering the wilderness. A billion diamonds lighten the dark sky as winds gust at tremendous speed; Kevin loses his hold on Brandon's hand. Below the clouds, forest fires rage from a solar storm and the moon's magnetic power striking through deforested habitats in cyclonic motion. Kevin screams, feeling gravity dropping five thousand feet through discharging clouds and mountains seen below!

Five hundred feet in midair, a flatland, seconds away from making a rough landing, hits the ground fast like an airplane in rapid descent! Kevin crashes into a bush and his entire body is stitched with many thorns. Comes out prickly, and the moon fades behind the sun. The moon eclipse ends! Will alien galaxies invade Planet Earth?

Brandon is gone. Kevin cannot walk or stand from motion sickness and falls on the farmland unconscious. Hopelessness jeopardized his survival. Kevin tried to save Brandon's life.

Never taught by anyone to be a brave survivor saving the world from collapse; civilization is on its knees when Mother Nature could destroy Earth's living organisms. Aliens might come from the moon to invade our planet. No one can stop them!

Kevin wakes up lying on the farmland surrounded by dense fog, and stands up ready to head back to Los Angeles, guessing which direction to move. A troublesome question for a lost survivor with no defence mechanism.

Trips over large pumpkins, trouble figuring out north, south, east, or west. No sunlight and strange climate. Imagines the consequences of following the wrong directions. Kevin walks through the fog. It's humid after the moon eclipse, where heavy smoke vapours from the burned ground. Dead animals everywhere—fallen trees and fragmented agricultural fields. Beyond, cumulus clouds form not far. Hopes it will rain.

Kevin crosses a burned landscape dressed in a winter jacket, a pair of running shoes, and no hat; walks in sweat, dying from thirst, heads towards an unknown direction where danger is difficult to see within this dark setting of sporadic fire. The challenge is to make it back to Los Angeles soon.

Gusty winds blow the skies away as a positive sign of calm weather. Great news, the world changes after the moon eclipse struck Earth. A spectacular but dangerous phenomenon!

Nowhere else to hide, an awful sense. Kevin will not make any stopovers till he reaches Los Angeles. A wise decision. Approaches the mainland, looking at a deforested landscape, nothing to feed himself, scared of dying, with no idea of which place he's hiding.

Having survived the moon eclipse, Kevin faces a long journey, to make it to Los Angeles early to save the millions of lives at stake. A dream to be a brave American survivor unafraid of danger and stay strong to fight the horrors of this strange world. One must prove oneself to be the hero who makes it to Los Angeles and rebuild the city brick by brick!

Kevin walks on a degraded landscape and jumps over a splitting ground. Nothing will stop him from taking the last chances to protect himself from Earth's violent powers. A sinkhole beside an abandoned train station. Kevin approaches, taking precautions, pays close attention to every step he makes, and watches for followers. Taking life-risk on his own, he never stops but he fears danger.

Kevin looks both ways, confused. Tough choices have pre-empted him to think fast and prepare for the unexpected. His weak vision makes it difficult to glance beyond the horizon where no light is eerie. Earth orbits closer to the moon. Kevin will be the one to face the apocalypse alone one day. The moon will someday replace Planet Earth. Soon, no one may live to see the universe disasters in human civilization. Sad ideas remind a catastrophe is near. Kevin is the last survivor desolated within an extinct world.

He drove the dump truck on this same path. Speed-walking, the road shakes! From nowhere, a freight train passes a metre away. Kevin jumps, makes it on top! Focused, trying to put terrible memories behind, thinking how to save Los Angeles from another disaster. Hours later, wakes up to see the sign "Welcome to Los Angeles" and no city to his left. Everything is dead, no people, but Kevin!

Kevin jumps off, skips the track, where he sees a bridge. Remembers this is the station where he took the 105 train to work. Runs to the bridge, sees the destroyed railroad and trains derailed, over a hundred passengers lie dead. Kevin follows this path, which takes him to downtown, and witnesses the ultimate destruction. Too late to save the world!

Wanders downtown Los Angeles under freezing temperatures. Where are the tall buildings? LA turns into a deserted place for no celebrities. Kevin stares at the grey skies. The moon has replaced Planet Earth. Frozen seagulls lie dead on the curbed street, restaurants and coffee shops burned to dust. Kevin faces the worst beginning of the twenty-first century. The moon eclipse caused the sun to orbit, the moon is Earth's twin planet, and nothing will bring civilization back. Human souls are dead and organisms have gone to extinction.

Chapter 2

The Curse of Notre Dame

Gendarmes guard the cathedral; inside the hallway, chandeliers lighten dark corners of the cathedral; above, the glass paintings make a stunning reflection of Christ. Everything is quiet. Luc is a priest and prays. After finishing his prayers, he approaches the doors and a crowd of prisoners pushes Luc—sprawls on the floor, watches them stealing treasures. The chandeliers slam on the ceramic floor and glass shatters into pieces. The holy paintings of the Virgin Mary and the angels from heaven, ruined. Luc does not stop them and reacts in anger.

The place becomes worse as gargoyles fly in, shattering windows. Luc goes up the spiral staircase in Notre Dame to give his respects and pray to God in the North Tower. He runs through the violent prisoners, reaching the open doors of the treasury room, sheltering himself; stands on the spot in shock, seeing every ancient treasure stolen, ripped paintings, and each broken statue lying on the wooden floor. Locks the door fast and hides under an antique chair made from gold. Luc hears a loud slamming on the door, looks at a small window—squeezing through it, taking his last chance for an escape; jumps out. Behind, Notre Dame is in flames!

Outside, the red eyes of gargoyles flare lasers, the same as a fire-breathing dragon. Luc puts himself in the position to save Paris on his own, apart from weak confidence. A terrible shock to watch Notre Dame burn to the ground. Luc runs on the empty streets; ahead, a plume of fog spreads and everything looks pitch dark. The streetlights have lost electricity at every corner.

The Mystery of Notre Dame

Luc falls on the cobble street and faints on the spot. Wakes up the next morning, finding himself situated beside a meat shop, the crowd rushing in fear, follows them. Ten minutes later, a disaster ahead, dark smoke fills the air with toxic smell, difficult for others to breathe! Remembers yesterday's horrifying scenes of prisoners stealing precious items and destroying their religious place, the House of God.

The king's musketeers stand in front of Notre Dame, confused. How did this happen? Paris faces its verge of collapse after many centuries since the English invasion. As a priest with a distinct nature to find truth, Luc looks around Notre Dame, searching for the gargoyles—passes through the enormous crowd and sneaks behind the soldiers. Runs towards the eastern section of Notre Dame. A few metres away, many dead prisoners lie in the parking lot. Finds a magnificent painting of the Virgin Mary ripped apart!

Poverty wrecked Paris. Citizens have no food to survive immuno-logical diseases. The destruction of Notre Dame! Broken antiques lying on the wooden floor. Luc sits on the ground, and has a brilliant plan to treasure hunt. Stands up and walks away from Notre Dame, heading towards the Bastille to find those prisoners who stole the antiques. After gunfire and cannonball shots, walks along the gutter between shops and old buildings, looking at the ruins of mass destruction. Impoverishment led to Paris in alienation.

No one knew Paris would turn into a violent city of deadly conflicts and mass-spread killings. Destroyed from the "City of Love" to torture. Luc's gifted imagination puts him in a sound position to stop riots and empower the unprivileged to stand up for their rights against corruption. Will he save Paris from bloodshed?

Close to the Bastille, a young boy steals sausages from a meat shop and the butcher yells, "Thief!" A soldier shoots the boy where everyone stands as eyewitnesses. A mother rushes over to her son, screaming, "Murderers!" Luc cannot watch the suffering of innocent people. It will be difficult for witnesses to forget today's tragic incident.

Luc dreamed of one day becoming a detective to search for clues and find Notre Dame's missing treasures. Looks around, and buildings fall. Families have no money. Luc passes beside beggars, seeing them suffer—the spoils of war and hunger. It makes him sad about days of starvation. He realized the Bastille prisoners stole treasures from Notre Dame to fight against corruption and protest the harsh revolution of King Louis's disinterests in the future of French people.

Paris in Danger

On a late afternoon, Luc finds himself within an impoverished world surrounded by brutality, alienation, and the homeless subjected to torture. Across the road, an old man stares at Luc as somebody whom he knew. The old man bows on Luc's shoes, begs for a blessing. Recites in a silent praise. Unpleasant animal sounds of angry gorillas raging as stampeding bulls destroy the streets of Paris. They run for their lives, and a big gorilla jumps over them in an attack and the road splits; the gorilla chews the homeless man.

Running towards the fountain, gorillas rage through churches and old buildings; behind, many dead bodies lying on the cobble street. Walking in beast footsteps, Luc never expected this to have such a terrible impact on France. This is the beginning. France will change into a dangerous place of no mercy and death. Monsters invade, killing every person alive, including innocent women and children; death tolls will rise, leading to one of the greatest disasters in the world's history.

No chance of finding the missing gargoyles. France is in danger of being annihilated by the alien invasion! Any chance of leaving this place alive? Citizens are not strong enough to win this war. Creatures coming from another planet to invade Paris. When the city burns, Luc will see a bloody sky filled with ash from the dead.

No hope. Despair is at every corner of the devastated streets of Paris—the lovely city under deep rubble. Stumbling over dead bodies, seeing the remains of lost children, Luc wanders in tears as darkness shuts his soul. Cannot save Paris from terrible threats. Families mourn for their loved ones in misery and are late for an escape. Luc is the one priest in Paris striving to survive in this treacherous world.

Luc spent hours thinking and walks along the streets of Paris's destruction, seeing the ashes from dead bodies. It is evening. No other place to pray and churches buried under deep ruins. Much worse, the Eiffel Tower collapses!

Luc imagines in his negative thoughts the dangerous turning points which might happen in the short term; meanwhile, going for a long walk, trapped within the estranged evil world. It makes no sense that slaves are fighting for their own lives while the king's musketeers are hiding inside the palace, afraid to go out.

Luc walks on spilled blood along the sidewalk. A bright red flash makes him lose consciousness; after regaining vision, he runs towards its path; a familiar sound, coming from a precise location not too far from a church. Four hundred metres away, Notre Dame blazes in flames and the streets split.

Witnesses rush to Notre Dame, battling the flames. The fire spreads, destroying homes, grocery markets, and churches. Luc never encountered such a terrible event in his life. Awful thoughts remind the worst is yet to come.

Approaches Notre Dame. Heavy smoke pollutes the environment; villagers on the ground suffocating. Out of nowhere, ghosts come flying through the flames scaring the living hell out of everyone, and Luc runs from death. Many dead people sucked in through the dark clouds. Paris turns into a haunted place, from love to torture.

Luc knows of a safe hideout place called Moulin Rouge. In his spirits, a fast runner to escape danger. No chance of saving others. The curse turns every person into dangerous evil man-eating cyborgs when ghosts come from Notre Dame in a rampage.

Finding a place to hide from these horrifying monsters, no one around, fear makes Luc's face sweat as he glances, keeping an eye for danger. Surrounded between a church and a meat shop, red-eyed stray dogs attack Luc and he grabs a frying pan, hitting both in the head. Out of nowhere, somebody comes to his rescue! An escaped prisoner from the Bastille, strangled in shackles, who stole Notre Dame's treasures!

Reaches for his pistol as two red-eyed stray dogs jump high and takes a clean shot, shooting at both as they fall on the ground, bleeding. The fight is over and this prisoner stares at Luc funny, preoccupied by this stranger who could be dangerous. This scares Luc! The prisoner comes, gives his hand, and pulls up Luc.

The prisoner speaks in a French accent. "Are you all right?"

Luc responds, "Yes. Thank you for saving me! What is your name?"

"My name is Alexandre."

"I am Luc. Nice to meet you!"

Alexandre grabs Luc, running towards a narrow corridor, the streets infested with rats; the crucifying image of Paris as victims are tortured to death; a young mother carries her baby. They couldn't watch innocent people suffer.

A Sad Ending

Hoping for water to ease their thirst, in front, a tall fountain. They found no water! Looking in both directions, famine deteriorates Paris, and no place of safe hiding. Terrible news. Trapped within a maze, Luc and Alexandre cannot climb the massive wall to reach the top. No exit signs, a dead end!

They fail to face new challenges and the last people alive in Paris fighting to survive against mass slaughter. It disheartens them to witness the collapse of Paris. The entire city faces a dangerous apocalypse much too soon! The risks are greater than being captured by spooky ghosts and wild animal beasts. The French nation cannot recover as other invasive organisms bring deadly wars to Planet Earth. No chance to make an escape.

Luc calls, "Alexandre, I found a ladder!" Brings the ladder, and places it on the north side where they will run on the narrow street.

Luc orders Alexandre, "I will climb it to check if it's strong." Makes it to the top.

Luc shouts, "Your turn, Alexandre! Do not worry, you can do it!"

Bending, Luc gives his hand to help Alexandre, and they make it! Sitting on top of this massive wall, seeing Paris in ruins, fires spread through homes, and they are alive amongst the millions deceased. They can't watch the bloodshed; tears in their eyes. Their homes no longer exist, and no other place to hide within this hopeless dystopian world as cyborgs destroy humanity. Cataclysm is everywhere!

Turning around, facing west, they see nothing except the remains of mass destruction of Paris's historical monuments. No choice but to move elsewhere. They will head east. On the other side of the wall, they descend, making their way towards deep rubble through heavy smoke, seeing no light and no other place to hide out from unexpected danger. Their current location is much worse. The flames taper along with signs of any shortcut to leave this horrible and depressing setting. Paris is a lost city, the ruins of old Europe.

It depresses them to leave Paris behind in the ashes. This is their chance to free themselves before they both die! Paying attention, they run, not looking at blood from dead bodies. Beyond fallen debris, they see a few men, one carrying an injured child, who run to shield themselves from the burning city. They move fast; trying to catch them is their ticket to flee. Approaching, Luc and Alexandre catch them!

Alexandre asking, "Guys, we are outcast trouble finding a way out. Can you help us and we will survive together? What do you think?"

The man carrying his child introduces himself as Jacques and speaks,

"All right. Follow me!"

Alexandre acquaints, "Jacques, my friend, Luc."

Following Jacques, they are the last survivors. Paris burns in flames, the pain inside their hearts, saddened by children dying with their parents, a shame to witness lost lives as they forget their own religion.

Survival is impossible. Leaping over the rubble blockade of bricks from the fallen Notre Dame, they help, take each other by the hand, head north-east behind the cathedral, the way out. At last, they make it!

No food to feed themselves and sad to watch the starving child crying about her deceased mother. A long journey is ahead. They walk within the dark areas of the forest in mud. They don't know where they are. As brave survivors, they understand it's a matter of time for a happy ending to come while they move forward in the same direction, not stopping. Jacques carries his dying daughter, and Luc feels sad with no strength to help.

Walking through foggy conditions above a burning sky; thick smog spreads fast and they see nothing but breathe the dry air. We will soon die! Luc thinks. He asks himself, Do I have the power as a brave survivor to lead these peoples out from this ugly forest?

No matter what happens, they'll do whatever it takes to get through this terrible setting. No leader. Luc has the chance to become one by proving himself he can save everyone from any unexpected attack. Nothing ahead. Everywhere is damp, smoggy, and unpleasant. Scarce trees make it impossible to figure out the wind's direction. They find themselves lost within a foreboding forest—too dry, pathless, and dangerous.

The group walks over big logs scattered around degraded areas, spotting no animals. Poisonous plants everywhere, and no sign of any human footprint, they have fewer chances of surviving in this sombre setting where is no place for Jacques' daughter. Hearing scary sounds, they move forward, ahead of the unknown. Surrounded by fallen oak trees, they are stuck wandering within a burned forest after a wildfire. There is no way back.

Luc is frustrated to hear the quarrels between Alexandre and Jacques. Luc stops the fight, and takes Alexandre with him as old buddies, leaving the others behind in farewell; one goes the other way.

Chapter 3

The Destruction of Nagasaki

I am Kenji. Two large sailing ships fire cannonballs at my home! I run to save many lives from being lost. Trapped within the overcrowded streets, scared of dying, I can't imagine the tragedies of hostility. Glancing from far, English soldiers are at the harbour on their ships armed with heavy ammunition, and a general sitting on his horse yells, "Move forward!" At a close distance, I witness the ruthless army seizing innocent families and grabbing children's arms!

A sumo wrestler fights two soldiers, and from behind, a colonel shoots him! It terrifies witnesses where I stand watching the innocent die. It is too late to save anyone. European colonization has killed many. The war has started. English soldiers bringing their ammunition in wooden barrels over to an abandoned sushi restaurant, and I see such a disgrace of the army throwing dead bodies into the water! I grab an axe, approach one young soldier, and swing it, hitting his lower abdomen, and spit on him! He deserved it.

Something strikes me from behind, and I fall on the pier. I gain consciousness on a torture chair with shackles around my wrists and both legs. A group of annoying soldiers approach, punching me in the face as blood drips from my nose and I hear them shouting at me. Close to breaking free in a fight to hit and teach them a moral lesson, I react in my language as they laugh at me, misunderstanding a word.

Out of nowhere, a group of samurai come through the window, attacking these soldiers with power and they lie dead! The samurai entangles me in these ropes and puts me on a horse, leaving Nagasaki behind in flames. I sit on the horse which gallops fast towards a deciduous forest, and I close my eyes, grasping the reins with both hands, holding my balance to prevent myself from falling. I duck, not to be hit by the loosened branches.

On the horse heading nowhere, I am taken to a small village somewhere in the hillsides of Hoshitoge no Tanada. After many miles of horseback riding along the grassy field, my knees ache from this long travel, which makes me desperate for a rest.

The villagers run towards me and a samurai, dressed in a dark-silver armour, grabs me, pushing me to a vernacular house called the Minka. Inside, a samurai lord known as the shogun governs laws and customs of this village. Crouched, he sits on the wooden floor eating his bowl of rice and vegetables.

The shogun speaks. "Who are you?"

I respond, "I am Kenji. Your men brought me here for no good reason. What do you want from me?"

"What is happening in your country?" the shogun questions me.

I say, "The Europeans are invading my country and killing many of my people. It is chaos! Many of us are living in the times of 'isolationism' and the English are making Japan into a nation of Western laws which govern trade between European countries."

The shogun replies, "I am Hiroto. I welcome you to my family, and you will learn the ways of a samurai!"

He looks at me, shocked, as the nation faces disparity and slaughter. This talk silences him. Surviving alone within this camp, surrounded by powerful fighters, I cannot imagine if they will hit me. This scares me as an inexperienced martial arts fighter.

Escorted by the shogun's housekeeper from the Minka to my home, I look around in fear, nervous about adaptation, not used to local customs; afraid one of the samurai will make fun of me or torture me if I don't learn their culture. The world differs from back home. Many duties have to be done, otherwise I'll enjoy less freedom! Approaching my large tent, not a Minka, I am curious if this place is safe to sleep away from ninjas.

My first night sleeping in the fields, I have no food and no water. It upsets me being in outcast. I experience the dreadfulness of remembering the bloodshed; I cannot afford to forget the death of my people. Revenge will one day be mine!

The next morning, I wake up to two samurai surrounding me as they stare at me with suspicion as an outsider. I remained quiet till one of them grabs me by my injured right arm, bringing me to the paddy fields; someone pushes me into the water and everyone laughs at me, and one of them throws a heavy shovel right in front of me. Never witnessing such cruelty of a samurai with no respect to foreigners, which displeases me.

Squatting on the grass covered in mud, sad to be treated as a pig, I am left in isolation. I give up and go back to my place in wet filthy clothes, the last clothes I have besides my old wool blanket.

It is time to teach those bastards a lesson—never to touch me again. Every day, I practice my wushu, remembering the techniques learned from the Master, a powerful man undefeated and the greatest fighter in Japan. Everyone called him "The Young Tiger." No one dared to challenge him. I wish to become a better martial artist.

For days, I study the key aspects of self-defence, training myself to be a street fighter as a self-centred person interested in real fighting. Every day, I spend hours examining my surroundings to keep clowns from harassing me. I was brought here as a slave to learn the ways of a samurai.

I grew up a disciplined child learning to write calligraphy; my self-control taught me to never react to bullies. I think "hold your ground" is a samurai's main discipline to fight with power. If someone interferes with my business or makes fun of me, I will let no one humiliate me in front of others; whatever it takes to straighten the problems and make this never happen again in my presence! I don't tolerate idiots inferior to me.

One sunny afternoon while working in the rice fields with villagers, the same bullies attack me in aggression. I stand on the spot, nervous with no weapon, recalling the flashbacks of demonstrating karate in front of the entire class; this suddenly gives me the energy to act fast, protecting myself from being hit by a shovel. I punch them and they fall over a steep hill. I defeat the enemy for the first time.

Practicing wushu at dawn; meditation helps my spirits follow the true path of becoming a master. For months, a samurai named Tung trains me in the main disciplines in advanced martial arts and shooting arrows against fierce enemies. I will always keep strong by defending myself from any attack. The others see my bravery and strength. I fight with my might and speed as a brave man. I never thought I could show fighting skill with no fear or hesitancy.

Working in the rice fields alone, I concentrate on my progress in learning to cultivate. My master trains me to become a powerful warrior ready for war and to fight against fearless soldiers. Every day, I become stronger with enormous fists. Someday, my teacher will tell me to do a small favour: to watch over his family till he comes back from battle, for which I am thankful.

I must prepare myself for any conflict. Meanwhile, I should think of other ways to improve my intuition before an army comes and destroys the village. This is a hard task for someone who has never fought in a battle.

The day of my first fight I win; everyone looks at me as I possess talents. It amuses me as a foreigner; not speaking their language made me think of myself as an outsider brought into this village where tough discipline requires effort. The challenge of being a samurai watching for his children is the tough part of life, which I must face!

A samurai must defend oneself during Japan's Edo Period—the dangerous times of impoverishment and isolation between people. It makes sense. I need to practice my horse riding before going to the battlefield alone. I have the power to protect my people. Remembering my grandfather, a war veteran who fought in the Boshin War against the shogunal forces when Japan was governed under Western powers. The world has become worse and more dangerous from many years of wars. I knew it would be hard to change the harsh reality of Edo Japan. My father will be proud of me if I do this for his honour and survive in a dying war before glory.

I must fight to prepare for war, either win or surrender. My master taught me never to take up arms to make yourself superior to others. For months of being encamped within this village, I understood retribution is our way as samurai for taking revenge for those we loved. This is important for us to recognize the patrimony of our beliefs.

Every samurai living within this world of desolation remembers the spoils of colonization. My days are ending. I will leave this village and head for Nagasaki, I don't know how this will turnout for me if I stay longer. For the past year, I have been working in the rice fields and practicing my fighting skills with a katana sword. I never knew I could manage this alone. I empower myself to gain knowledge of people's oral traditions and understand the roots of a samurai.

A wintry day within the village where the rice fields are in deep freeze of extreme frigid temperatures and water shortage. Someone warned me the ninjas will come and we need to prepare fast. I am strong to take life risks.

Gathering the weapons, for days we practice wushu in the fields as a fighting group. Everyone is confident we will win, making ourselves powerful men. We brave warriors will fight to the death to protect our country from destruction and save the lives of children. It is our custom; we choose as samurai to fight for our survival and to prepare a vast army of young fighters by joining in alliance with professional archers.

We gather the wood and cover the corners of our homes with bamboo logs, which will keep us safe in case they fire explosives. I think the war with the ninjas will soon happen as we are ready to fight, waiting until they come and invade our village. Everyone sits inside the temple meditating in their prayers, facing the statue of Buddha. We hear thunder rumbling outside and the heavy rain dripping from the rooftop.

Everyone sleeps except for me. I step out, looking at the rain. I take the chance wandering around and keeping watch for the enemy to warn the villagers if an attack happens. I hear a frightful scream of raging ninjas running through the open fields as fierce barbarians, and I shout in Japanese, "Ninja," waking everyone.

I witness the panicking of my people as they grab swords, rushing outside in the fight against fifty ninjas! Dashing through the temple with my katana, ready to kill ninjas, my feet are soaking wet from the drenching rainfall and strong winds blow large rain droplets at me. The ground shakes from close lightning strikes! Under my waraji, I notice blood making my socks red. My master's dead body drifts away in torrential rain and I'm in shock, fearing this might be the end for me!

Out of nowhere, a raging ninja runs straight towards me as I grab my katana, swinging it and cutting through the ninja's armour, and blood splatters on my face! I have won! The rain stops, and I stroll, seeing many dead samurai and ninja bodies lying on the ground, brutalized by war. I hear no sounds, having no place to go. I have to leave this place and save myself from death.

Leaving Hoshitoge no Tanada, I walk on dead samurai bodies, looking through the fog as my face sweats from a burning tree struck by a thunderbolt. It depresses me as a survivor alienated within a treacherous world, feeling no motivation to head further. This journey continues to be challenging and unpredictable. If I make stupid mistakes, putting my life in danger, I have no other choice but to abandon this village to return home. I cannot imagine this long way by foot without a horse.

Walking across the flooded escarpment, holding my katana sword, paying close attention to my surroundings—too quiet and dark for a samurai who doesn't know where else to go. I am left an outcast trying to find the direction of my hometown while searching for food and a safe place to stay till morning. I can't help it!

My senses tell me to follow the hills, finding available resources for eating, and to be cautious which foods to pick. I know Japan's hillsides encompass natural wonders by observing wild animals. A lucky opportunity for a quick hunt.

I see no sunset and darkness everywhere; tripping over a big rock, hit with loss of cognition and no visual. My whereabouts are pitch black. I fall asleep, tired from walking in the middle of nowhere. The next morning, I wake up somewhere unknown asking myself, Where am I? Good question.

Surrounded by cattle and horses, it reminds me of being near a farm. Japanese farmers look at me, guessing I am an outlaw. Who brought me to this strange setting? Making an escape is risky for me, not knowing the consequences of starvation. I cannot imagine the impact. Surviving this tough reality as a foreign outcast with nothing except my sword and fighting skills, I have doubts whether I can do this alone.

Sitting on the hay, I think of other ways to plan my journey before it is too late for taking risks. Tough decisions blanket my mind with the wrong intentions of surviving on my own, with no experience of fighting professional soldiers. I decide to leave this place before the winds change. Quick thinking! I see no one, taking my last chances to make an escape, running towards the forest through the narrow corridor. Avoiding death while experiencing leg pain, I cannot afford to make a rest stop, and my challenge upon arriving in Nagasaki is to rescue my peoples from terror. This quest puts me in a dangerous position where I am surrounded by ferocious animals.

Am I headed in the right direction back to my hometown? Confused with no solution and negative thoughts bother me most as I run away in the middle of nowhere. I come closer to seeing people being shot, and I hear gunfire and cannonball shots. Back in Nagasaki, the English march, killing many people. What might happen tomorrow? Will the one samurai with no army fight the English? The insanity of this life-ending drama puts me in a tragedy. I cannot imagine the consequences of dying as the last warrior. I look around and see bloodshed, the screaming of innocent children, mothers and fathers killed in action, homes and temples destroyed; lost lives for the cost of war. Ashamed of myself that I cannot save lives.

I cannot stop thinking of being a hero saving the world. Not much time to learn new skills and no full army of samurai leading them inside Nagasaki. My country is turning into a nation of extremism. Edo, a political state of imperialism, countries becoming allies with the English. It is crazy to kill thousands of English soldiers in one day with no weapons! I knew this would happen. I will not give up my personal vendetta. Never seen the English general and don't know his real name.

I remember buying fish and vegetables with my parents at the food market; this changed. Stores close, and poverty. Japan has become too desperate for families. Nothing can be done!

A young samurai with no hiding place. I am facing a disaster, with no war party to fight ruthless soldiers. My people are encamped in training to become superhuman; I have less time to prepare myself for the worst. This is madness!

How will I fight the whole English army with no weapons or warriors? Angry, not ready to serve in war, I cannot support my nation as a Japanese warrior who does not realize the challenges of preparing for battle. I cannot imagine the glory of dying in front of the firing machine guns.

I throw my sword, crying, the utter hopelessness inside me—cannot defend myself against the enemy. Imaging I am on the battlefield leading the army on a galloping horse in a furious attack to kill soldiers. In front of me, a raging general runs wild towards me with his revolver shooting in close range and I swing my sword, splitting his head in two! Blood splatters my armour and face!

I wake up in shock lying on the dirty ground covered in dust within the cesspool of inhumanity. I have the power to win battles by proving myself the best amongst armies. One day, I hope I will be a samurai who shows no fear, with strength to prove I can fight.

To save my people from further bloodshed is to leave for the upper territories. My quest is to end this war by heading north to find more men to accompany my return to Nagasaki.

Out of nowhere, a runaway horse approaches and neighs beside me! A fine animal! I sit on it. "Trot!" Gallops across the street heading towards the small degraded forest, through the ashes of burned trees where fire surrounds me. Trapped in the centre, surrounded by burning bushes—on the count of three—I prepare myself, can't tell the height, afraid of losing my balance. I take a chance, holding the reins tight with both hands and sitting on the saddle in a stiff position, keeping my posture steady. The horse gallops fast as I close my eyes, the wall below me; making a rough landing as I rejoice, saving myself from danger. I pet the horse. "Good boy!"

Heading northeast of Hoshitoge no Tanada. I don't know what will happen if my horse dies, walking in the middle of nowhere. Journeying through the battlefield, seeing heavy artilleries and many soldiers sitting on the ground having their meal. The others suspect me in their territory. The horse gallops faster to avoid being caught in an ambush. Beyond the hillside, I see oxen, and butterflies fly over me, a sign I am near a ripe plantation. Hungry for food.

Horse-riding with no break, fearing being captured, I am not comfortable surviving alone with nothing. My tolerance is rock-bottom. Thinking whether to stop for food or continue heading further along the rice fields, I don't know how will I find the place I'm looking for if the weather changes. Questioning myself, am I aware of my physical whereabouts? I need to still figure this out. No time, I don't have the stomach to carry out my duty! My false judgements irritate me above all other misfortunes I have been through since the moment the English war started in Nagasaki.

Sitting on the horse, I am bothered by the regrets of dying in war, which confuses me about whether to continue moving forward or return home. Lost in the wilderness, hopeless in despair, I under-estimated myself as a superhuman who never fought against an immense army. Japan's hero who can end this war with a full brigade of Japanese warriors. It hurts me. I am not ready for this fight.

As a martial arts student, I dreamed it was my future to become a great warrior. Fighting compromised my judgement. Something has changed in me. Idiosyncrasies clouded my perception and turned me into a person who is not ready to fight. Struggling to figure out directions, I see no home where survival is not a challenge. Nerve-racked to find food; war has shown its destruction on human existence.

Hopeless, death has given me a well-learned lesson never to abandon my home if I have no one to guide me; naïve and too quick, making the wrong decisions for my name to be carried out through the ages, proving myself inferior amongst powerful enemies. Is it the fight for redemption?

I've had enough! Above me, the sky spins; I jump off, lying on the ground screaming with such pain of abandoning my countryman! I experience vertigo after falling from my horse, hitting my back at top-speed, which ends in an injury.

Losing consciousness, looking ahead as my horse gallops away, I suffer from weakness which turns me into a weak superhuman, not strong. Moments later, I black out. I lie flat at verge of my death and no one here to save me. I went through a terrible experience with no hopes. Life has taught me a moral lesson: never go looking for trouble.

Lost in the wilderness, somewhere deserted within a place unknown in Japan, stuck on top of a mountain, or worse? Unconscious, feeling not alive. Damn me! Unawake for days, my mindset is affected by the horrors of war and killings of my people, who I have abandoned; sorrow breaks my heart, disheartens me too much above other worries besides the loss of freedom.

It has been a month of darkness and no sign of anyone. I wake up finding myself surrounded by warriors! I am sick to my stomach, having not eaten. Encamped in a war party within a dangerous setting of fierce warriors, reimagining myself in a different world.

Someone has placed the burning firewood beside me. Warmth comforts as I experience a fever, covered under a wool blanket in my clothes wet from sweat. I cannot speak from the pain in my lungs and body cramps. Given horrible medicine as a cure to my illness, sick for days and no sign of any improvement—lucky me, I am kept in this camp alive! Thanks to the generosity of these warm-hearted tribesmen.

I take a short walk, thinking to wander off on my own. I should not do this! The tribesman stare at me as a Japanese fighter from the uncivilized world. One approaches me, wanting to look at my sword, never seen a weapon of this kind before, talking amongst themselves in their language. I misunderstand a word. I let them borrow it and do not hesitate.

They stay in a circle surrounding me, suspicious-looking, an outsider from somewhere with a different fighting experience and from another culture. I rise in the centre, the tribe circling me. I do not make any sudden moves, afraid to take a piss. Everyone watches me, dressed in my silky-white clothes and my long hair never cut.

The warriors look at me, cynical; I am not a fighter. A muscular guy swings his big punch at me. I fall, hearing the laughter; I kick the bastard's face, throwing his spear away into the bushes and punch him hard and he flies a few metres ahead, hitting himself hard on the sand. The others looked stunned. They will never bother me again!

Proud of myself because I fought well with great skill, made a quick recovery after the terrible illness! I must set up a war party in the fight against terror and return absolutism to Japanese culture by ending corruption! This time, I won't fail to bring peace to my peoples. It will be difficult to train these warriors for battle.

The others walk away, and I sit on the ground thinking of establishing a battalion. I estimate around a hundred tribesmen trained to fight with different tactics. I will need to teach these warriors to use katana swords. To save Nagasaki from bloodshed, I must think of a brilliant solution to create a big company of fighters to attack the English army by force! It is my destiny to end this war. Will I succeed?

The next morning, I prepare the tribesmen for battle as I convince them Nagasaki is in devastation! In front of me, I see the soldiers gathering their archers and hunting rifles, which I've never seen, and this impressed me. These men bring more fighters, and it looks more than a hundred!

Aligning everyone for our march to Nagasaki, we paint our faces before going to battle as part of our tradition to win this war. I fear of no tomorrow and my mind tells me it will be a big fight; we have rifles and ammunition to kill and swords to defend ourselves.

My army marches across the grassland towards an abandoned village, seeing burned homes and dead farmers. We continued making our way through the dark forest, which will lead us to Nagasaki, depending on our pace as we advance. Hours later, it is nightfall and we are tired with little time for rest, no chance of camp. I fear losing over a hundred of my warriors and putting their lives at risk.

I command the entire army to go on running forward until we reach the open corridors downwind. We march along the pathways on mud through steam and the heavy smoke after gunfire. It's difficult for me to observe our current location. Nothing to lit fire, and no spot for sleeping, we hear the sounds of wild animals from a short distance.

We run for our lives to escape this dreadful setting and move forward in the same direction seeing a rainstorm in the face of us! Nowhere to hide! No choice but to lead ourselves through the drenching rain and powerful winds. The monsoon season. Forcing ourselves through this dangerous storm. My men, blown away by cyclonic winds and lightning bolts, fire the skies. Nagasaki is close.

Hours pass, the storm stops, and thunderclouds disappear. Daylight and cloudy skies are what we see. We look through the smoke at Nagasaki a mile away, see English soldiers and a large colony of the vast Spanish army routing the north gates! Running towards the battlefield, we grab our swords and arrows, screaming with our speed, spirit, showing the enemy our power.

A few of my men are dead. Heavy artilleries bombard us, trying to defend ourselves with everything we have left. Few weapons, unlucky! I doubt we'll win this war. It looks I will be the one superhuman to kill the English general with my powerful arm and proclaim victory. My true heart is to battle for justice by proving to myself I am the best warrior in Japan. Half of my army is dead, and I must kill for my survival. I am the last fighter to take revenge for my countrymen.

The others lie dead and I am the one standing beside a cannonball that is about to explode! Jumping on the horse with my strength, we gallop in revolt against the powerful general. I suspect him riding across the front line. He reaches for his revolver, shooting a few rounds at me, and I throw my sword from the back and kill him. He falls to the ground! Victory is mine, and the war is over as armies head back home. I am the last one resting on the battlefield where Nagasaki is in ruins.

I am a brave survivor, proven to be strong. The English army fears me and no one dares to challenge! It is a disappointment no armies will ever help us restore Nagasaki. Our heritage as Japanese peoples obliterated by devastating wars.

Wandering on the battlefield, seeing the English army have lost their fight, I am proud as a samurai who fought well on this historic day an end of the Edo Period. The corrupt Sakoku foreign policy is done. I watch the English soldiers I killed. The blood on my sword shows the past of destruction and bloodshed between armies. It is my custom to honour the dead, having the pride of respecting a fallen soldier after winning a battle.

My father once taught me: "Never hate your foes. A brilliant soldier fights with spirit and power and never takes sides against his own army."

I've thought of his last words since the moment I became samurai. I am a superhuman who fights for a country, bringing European colonization to an end. A brave and powerful warrior must show inferiority against ruthless kings. Wandering a long mile, I bring my battalion to Nagasaki and re-build this small town with the help of my comrades. I run back.

Commanding my men, I say, "We will march to restore my home. If you're with me, we will live together as a powerful nation of justice and equality! Are you with me?"

"Yes!" chants my company.

I order them to move forward, heading straight for Nagasaki! My army of seventy warriors march with me, happy. We have won the war; much more needs to be done before we proclaim full victory of our success.

Approaching the hillside, seeing Nagasaki from a close distance, a lost city and a dark desert of mass destruction deteriorated by hillsides. How will we restore this place? Everyone looks shocked to see the aftermath of war where thousands of bodies lie dead! We are the last brave peoples alive to re-populate.

We find nothing. The setting looks abandoned and destroyed by cannonballs. In a death world, everything is empty. No point of staying as one army of seventy men. We leave.

Marching through Nagasaki, watching innocent civilians die, we gather to pay our respects to the fallen; a funeral for the thousands of lives killed in action. No chance of rebuilding Nagasaki. Our custom is we never leave behind dead bodies to rot on the burning ground.

Divide ourselves in small groups of ten, turning Nagasaki into a graveyard. We never wanted it to end this way. Our opportunity to rebuild the new Nagasaki on the remains of lost survivors. Emotional to bury the dead on our home soil where we stand in tears, as few remember their loved ones who fought in this war, protected Nagasaki from bloodshed. We will never forget the history of our brave people.

Seeing my men taking dead bodies to their graves, I rub my eyes, go for a short walk to find my close relatives. I want to be alone in this moment of sadness, trying to remember the faces of my parents, brothers, sisters, cousins, nephews, and uncles. Been away for months. Everything changed after the last day of freedom.

A terrible experience for me to witness the slaughter of my innocent countrymen. My nose itches from smelling the pungent stench air. Coming to this place where I lived long ago, the door handle locked in chains, and a loosened arm appears right in front of me! Cannot recognize who is it, I pull the arm and the locks break! It is my baby brother, Hiroyuki. I take his body behind my back, bringing it over to the graveyard to bury his remains. Others stand in a moment of silence.

Chapter 4

The Criminal and The Lion

Today is the Battle of Teutoburg Forest in Kalkriese, Germany; the year 9AD, when the Caesars conquered the world to rule the empire! A soldier to lead the Romans into the heart of Rome, putting corruption to an end. Alexius will be the next Caesar to bring peace. His father is Isthmus Volucious, the greatest Caesar who conquered the Spanish army. The Roman Republican has expanded a political imperium throughout Europe. Alexius's brother Marcus will one day become general of the Roman army.

As a moral man, Alexius wanted to bring peace by honouring his father. Marcus and Alexius shared everything. Marcus looked much older than Alexius in his late twenties. Marcus fought in many battles as a young soldier. He was well-experienced in war and killed enemies with his own strength. The greatest warrior. Everyone knew the dark soul of Marcus, jealous of his brother Alexius, who would take place as emperor.

The German army is moving in on the battlefield, and the Roman army is coming closer. Marcus waits for a red flag to lead his men towards the danger zone. The moment comes!

Marcus shouts, "Move forward!"

Below a grey sky, Roman soldiers run towards open fire, and the barbarians come out from the bushes attacking them with their fierce swords. Many Roman soldiers are dead, as they were not ready for war. The Roman general sitting on his horse sees more soldiers are dying and the army is on the verge of forfeiting this battle with no backup! Right on time, Marcus's men come and destroy the German army, killing the notorious general with a swing of his sword! He wins the battle!

Marcus walks around, seeing many deceased soldiers lying on the ashes. Nothing to breathe, blood filths the air from dead soldiers' remains, beech trees burned by stone-throwing carroballista, and fire blazes at every corner of the forest. The day of victory is marked as the remembrance of fallen Roman soldiers. Marcus steps on burned soil. His comrades greet and congratulate him.

Marcus stands in the middle of the battlefield waving his sword in front of the entire Roman army, where soldiers chant their victory. With a surprise, from nowhere, Alexius rides his horse together with his girl Ornella. Deep inside Marcus's black heart, he is angry as they approach him in a formal greeting; Marcus and Alexius both hug each other.

Ornella acquaints. "It is a pleasure to meet you."

Marcus responds, "You look charming, my lady. Alexius, I won the war!"

Alexius salutes, "Congratulations!"

Marcus keeps both Alexius and Ornella in good company as they walk towards the camp where the celebrations will be. Marcus sees Ornella kissing Alexius on the cheek. A love at first sight.

Every Roman soldier joins the Caesars and celebrates their victory against the Germans. Marcus, Ornella, and Alexius sit together as close friends, drinking wine while having a good time. Ornella and Alexius are both drunk, and Marcus knows the perfect moment for a silent kill! Alexius falls on the table losing consciousness and Marcus helps him up, taking his brother out for a breath of fresh air.

Marcus carries Alexius far away to a nearby forest—a perfect place to commit a crime. Approaching the battlefield through dense fog, Marcus drops Alexius on the ground, grabbing a knife from the pocket, and stabs him in the heart! Blood stains the dry soil.

Marcus puts the branches over Alexius's dead body to hide him and walks with blood on his hands. He sees the camp from a mile and throws the knife away. No place to have a bath. Marcus approaches and tiptoes inside a tent, lying beside someone tucked under a fur blanket. Coincidence, Marcus wakes up the next morning lying beside Ornella's naked body!

She awakens, yawning. "Alexius, is it daylight?"

Marcus surprises her. "Good morning, my love. I am your new husband!"

"Where is Alexius?" Ornella questions.

Putting someone else's armour on himself, Marcus responds, "I don't know—"

A screaming voice, "Alexius is dead!"

Ornella yells, "Murderer!!"

Marcus hides himself from the group, peeking from behind an outhouse, looking from a close distance. Ornella cries as she kisses Alexius's face. Marcus knows the pain inside her heart with no condolence. The soldier who became a criminal to his people and killed his brother for vengeance. It is tragic nothing will bring him back. Marcus approaches Ornella, hugging her, and listens to the quavering voice, "Hail, Caesar!" At the funeral, Ornella has pain inside her heart as she watches the burial of Alexius's body on the battlefield. Soldiers lead the ceremony. Marcus knows Ornella will miss Alexius till the time they meet again.

A few days later, Marcus becomes emperor of Rome. Heading for a long journey through desert and mountains towards Rome, leaving with the entire command from the Kalkriese camp, Ornella cries every day, which angers Marcus. He pays no attention to the lovely young woman who lost her husband; a lack of sympathy in a devil's heart!

Approaching the mainland; it is wintry weather, and everyone is surviving this blizzard, moving through blowing snow and strong winds. Many soldiers were left behind to their death after the storm.

On the fourth morning, we make it through the mountains, passing the Sahara Desert approaching Morocco's capital, Marrakech. Upon arrival, others watch us, thinking we are outsiders who have come to invade their country. We continue our journey through the city with no stop and we witness poverty. From nowhere, an Arab comes to Ornella begging for money, and she tells the soldiers to stop for a quick second. Deep inside her heart, Ornella feels sorry for this beggar and takes her chance to help.

Marcus throws a rock at him and yells, "Move away, you dirty old man!"

Ornella shouts, "Marcus, what on earth are you doing?"

He looks funnily at Ornella's generosity. She gives the coins to the Arab, and the army continues to march towards the gates. She knows Marcus will never make friends.

An army of powerful men leads us from Marrakech. Ornella and Marcus travel across the Sahara Desert in their Roman litter, crossing Spain's anterior. No water. Ornella worries this journey will become worse if we lose our army. We do not leave our men to die!

Moving through the narrow corridor, Marcus is sound asleep and Ornella peaks through the curtains, seeing a line of trees where sunlight touches the northeast side. Reaching the mountain slope at low elevation where Ornella sees Rome from a close distance!

Ornella wakes up Marcus. "We made it! See for yourself." His eyes opened, hears a large volume of people from far!

Up ahead, coming closer to the centre of the city, Marcus and Ornella both tell the soldiers to stop. An enormous crowd makes it hard for the eight of us to pass. Marcus and Ornella are riding with a Roman charioteer.

A few senators greet Marcus and Ornella. "My Lord, Mistress, welcome to Rome. We are happy to see you as our future emperor to this nation!"

One day, Marcus will be emperor to govern Rome, but not Ornella. It becomes obvious he must show his fighting skill in the Colosseum, where battles will happen tomorrow. Ornella cannot wait till the day Marcus becomes the winner to honour his father's wishes. We enter the gates, heading towards the palace and accompanied by powerful men. People throw rose petals at us! A warm welcome. A pleasure to be united with a powerful republic.

The charioteer stops. Marcus and Ornella share hands, walking towards three senators. They kiss her hand. Marcus interrupts, "Excuse me, Senator, she's with me." Ornella is mad at Marcus for acting vulgar in front of everyone.

After a long journey, Ornella goes to her room to nap, and the senators speak frankly with Marcus inside the large chamber to discuss politics and issues.

Senator Darcus addresses. "We need to discuss the social problems which Rome has."

Marcus responds, "Senator, this nation deserves a powerful emperor with guts and vision. Someone to make new laws for the future of Rome where everyone will live free."

Marcus leaves the chamber. The senators look at him wrong despite his jealousy as a misanthrope. Marcus opens the door to Ornella's room and throws his sword and toga on the bed and falls asleep dreaming about his brother's death.

The next morning, Marcus and Ornella are both awake, ready for today's wedding ceremony held at the Colosseum. An exciting day for Marcus being promoted as Rome's Second Emperor and Ornella to be married with him as his empress. Will this be their destiny? They prepare themselves for this ceremony, saying no words, then the guards escort them to the chariot. No crowd on the streets. They are waiting for us to arrive. A half-hour later, we make it inside the Colosseum.

Hearing the crowd chanting, "Caesar! Caesar! Caesar! We are here to salute you!"

A spokesperson presents, "Bow to your new emperor!"

Everyone shouts, "Hail, Caesar!" Marcus looks surprised.

Praetorian Guards surround Marcus and Ornella, where they both stand in the centre. A priest is in front of them; gladiators run towards Marcus and Ornella. Their last chance to escape! At the right time, the Praetorian Guards rush over to save them from danger! Fierce gladiators dominate the arena to fight in glory against the Egyptians.

At the perfect moment, with a magnificent view, Marcus and Ornella both sit watching their first gladiator match. The crowd stands in a loud applause! Marcus had never seen a gladiator match before and thinks he wants to become one. An interesting perspective for a criminal who's guilty of treason; honouring himself as emperor will soon be an end.

Marcus imagines himself as a stronger soldier than his brother Alexius. Marcus knows winning his first battle will contribute to him being the greatest warrior. His ego is brute and cannot rule. Ornella misses Alexius, the one lost but dear to her heart. She has given Marcus a second chance to prove himself he can be emperor as she wishes him the best. Can they live together without violence?

Marcus commands the gladiators to kill the Egyptians, and they win! The crowd chants; they enjoy the gladiator match. Ornella and Marcus return home after seeing their first tournament, and Marcus receives a waiver to be challenged in a duel. He laughs. Ornella looks at him as a selfish and unreasonable man, judging by his reaction. Married to someone with an evil heart and no sympathy for others, Ornella has chosen her own path. Marcus drops the waiver on the floor.

Ornella picks up the waiver, reads it:

"The strongest fighter in the world, the unbeatable Norian, invites you to a challenge."

Ornella knows Norian will beat Marcus. The gods as their witnesses. She has a warm-hearted nature and judges no one, always has respect for others. Marcus is asleep, and Ornella sits in the chamber alone, hoping that Norian will kill Marcus. Marcus must prove himself by beating the powerful enemy.

It is morning, the day of the fight of Marcus versus Norian from Africa! This battle can make it history! Ornella puts Alexius's armour on Marcus as good luck to honour her husband. Marcus grabs his armour with both hands and throws it on the floor.

Marcus yells at Ornella, "Never again mention the name Alexius in my presence! I am your emperor, your king!" Marcus leaves her behind where she stands in tears.

How rude of Marcus to treat a young and sensitive girl with disrespect. A madman who hates the world; thinks he is superior throughout the Roman empire. Ornella hates dangerous people as this emperor cares for no one. She decides not to watch Marcus fighting within the arena after what happened this morning.

Ornella looks through her window and sees Marcus lifting his sword high and the crowd chants, "Caesar." A tall man approaches Marcus, prepared for a fight! Moments later, Norian swings a powerful punch, striking Marcus, and he falls to the ground in humiliation. Ornella smiles as she watches him being beaten; out of nowhere, an unleashed lion charges Norian and attacks him from behind, saving Marcus's life! The crowd looks stunned to see a lion helping the emperor. The lion walks with Marcus, accompanying him back to the palace as his new best friend. Marcus walks, injured in his armour.

The Praetorian Guards exclaim, "Why did you bring this beast?"

Marcus says, "It saved my life today and nobody will touch him. Do you understand?"

"Yes, Caesar," they respond.

Marcus orders, "The lion will stay with me under my command, and I will name him Leonidas."

Ornella leaves with the guards, walking out the door. Marcus is left alone in the room with the lion lying flat on the floor. The animal roars beside him! Marcus doesn't pay attention to this pulse-pounding moment when the beast wants food, hopefully not him for breakfast! Ornella is never talking to Marcus anymore. He is in real trouble with dangerous company. The lion acts friendly despite Marcus's nasty personality; always a tough guy with no understanding of how to respect a woman.

Marcus has no clue where to find food to feed this hungry lion. Kill a person? Marcus masks himself, wears a Roman helmet as a disguise and grabs his knife before leaving outside, tiptoeing. It is the middle of the night, the perfect hour for a silent kill.

Marcus approaches an old man and stabs him in the back with his knife. The innocent man lies dead on the ground and Marcus looks around, seeing no witnesses. He carries the guy with both arms, rushing back to the palace before anyone catches him. Everyone is sound asleep.

Marcus ascends the staircase, keeping his balance strong to avoid a fall. The dead body drips blood on the carpet. At last, he reaches his room, laying the dead body on the floor, and strips clothes. The lion wakes up smelling blood and eats the body, chewing every bone on the skin with its powerful jaws! Marcus watches the lion eating the rest of the bodily remains, not scared. His evil nature! A real psycho, he is!

Marcus takes the carpet and throws it through the window, and it falls in a courtyard. The lion licks the spilled blood from the floor and is fast asleep and Marcus cleans his sword, as he stands awake throughout the night, fearing someone saw him.

The next morning, Marcus is sleeping, and the lion wakes him up roaring, startling him. He lies beside a skeleton and screams! A servant comes out and catches Marcus covered in blood! He glances around and stands up, running to Ornella's room, not finding her, and hears a commotion from outside and sees her arguing with a Roman soldier!

Marcus runs to them and shouts, "What is the commotion?"

Ornella screams, "Marcus, I saw you killed an old innocent man last night, Senator Bergius from our council! How could you do this to me?!"

The Roman soldier orders Marcus to show proof of the crime committed. Everyone rushes upstairs. Marcus smells of something dead. He sees Leonidas eating a dead body.

In anger, Ornella tries to threaten the lion to scram. It roars, jumps on her neck in an attack, chews off her neck as Marcus comes to rescue! Too late! She is dead! Marcus has no sympathy. The Praetorian Guards come and arrest Marcus for killing the old man, taking his pet away. By the orders of the Senate, they forced Marcus to leave Rome forever and never return!

The Praetorian Guards escort Marcus to the chariot, tangling his wrists with thick rope. The price Marcus must pay for what he has done. A disappointment, for Marcus committed many crimes! A shame for a young emperor, untrusted. Now, Rome is corrupt. Ornella gone. It will be difficult for the Senate to change without compromise.

Marcus is guilty of murder and they will sentence him to death. Halfway to the prison, Marcus wakes up and tries to escape, biting the rope around his wrists, and prepares himself before someone catches him. His strong teeth cut through the thick ropes for the chance to free himself! Marcus jumps off the chariot, runs towards a lion cage, and hides himself within, waiting till it's safe to head back. He sees people passing by. It's difficult to see if anyone is following him; he cannot risk being arrested. Marcus waits till dark, the perfect moment to move without being unnoticed by others.

Marcus sneaks in through an empty house and finds enough food to steal, taking much with him: a heavy load of dry fruit, water, wine, and meat. Marcus heads west to have something to eat before sunset. A smart idea for a gifted criminal who is surviving the hardships without Ornella.

Making a campfire while preparing his meal, Marcus sees Ornella's ghost through the fire, which reminds him of the mistakes he's made. He eats in silence. Marcus is full and falls asleep. He awakens the next morning, preparing himself for his return to Rome, many miles of heat ahead where trees are dead, no pond, or place to avoid the blistering sun. Desolation for Marcus surviving with no help.

The grazing sun shines above a desert landscape; no person has dared to make it across the death valley except for Marcus—a strong-looking fellow; an emperor who became an imprisoned man. It is time for Marcus to pay for his wrongdoings. A lesson never to ravage a country of his birth rite.

Making it to Rome faster than any army, Marcus approaches the front gates with nothing in his hands, coming as a free man to ask for forgiveness. Marcus returns to convince the senators to make him emperor after the crimes he committed. An apology is not enough.

Senator Darcus notices Marcus and questions him. "Why did you come back? You are not welcome anymore!"

Marcus speaks in a sad tone. "I am sorry for my wrongdoings. I want to become the new emperor. Please reconsider."

Senator Darcus confronts Marcus. "You killed an innocent man and betrayed your people. You are guilty of sedition and can no longer be the emperor. I don't want to see your face anymore. Take this man out of my sight!"

Marcus bursts into anger. "I will be back. Nothing will stop me! I will kill your new emperor!"

Marcus is locked inside the lower dungeon, strangled in chains.

Marcus puts his strength to free himself, entangling the shackles on both wrists. A strong man with guts! Marcus opens the door and walks, finding his way out before the guards catch him escaping. He goes through a narrow corridor towards the fences. Marcus climbs over it and jumps on the ground running for his life to break into the emperor's room and kill him!

Marcus reaches the palace and finds his path up the stairs. Inside the room, he sees the emperor sound asleep. Marcus picks up the chair and someone from behind kills Marcus, cutting through his body with a two-edged sword! Master Claudius saves the new emperor from assassination; a man more warm-hearted than the evil Marcus. Witnesses looked surprised. Tomorrow, Senator Darcus will invite Master Claudius to the Colosseum to appoint him as the new emperor, handing over his daughter Lucilla to be joined in marriage. An exciting time for them.

The next day, the senators watch the promotion ceremony, hoping Claudius will bring wealth to the people. The future Rome deserves a grateful emperor to create a scripture of laws to build a nation of liberty. Claudius, a brave man to save Rome from corruption. He has made history!

The senators congratulate Claudius. A gladiator hands a wooden sword to him as a gift. Claudius thanks them for it. He is married to Lucilla as the new emperor of Rome! The crowd applauds! Claudius and Lucilla both stand in the arena hearing "Hail, Caesar!" This day marks victory against the ruthless Marcus.

Chapter 5

Surviving Unimagined Dystopias

Moosetown, the place where my parents brought me up. From childhood to now, my first year in junior high, I've lived in the same old neighbourhood and enjoyed a normal life. This changed on June 07, 2022, the day of the catastrophe. In my room, I turned on the television and heard:

"Aliens will soon invade Earth, bringing dangerous climate to destroy us!"

"Is this a joke?" I reacted.

I ignored the broadcast and ate breakfast and went out for a short walk. The weather was gorgeous, sunny. Strolling a few blocks south from my house, I saw kids riding their bikes with families and friends, dog-walkers socializing with each other. I wished to meet up with my classmates for a fun time, to enjoy this pleasant day together. Not anymore. Thirty minutes later, approaching a nearby playground, I noticed the dark sky and the frightful sounds of crows flying above me. Suddenly, the park became a haunted forest as the storm turned cyclonic.

A horrible scream of aliens shook the sidewalk. Wolverines rushed through the park, destroying houses. I saved myself, climbing on a tall tree during the thunderstorm. My neighbours took their shotguns in an attack. The situation became worse. Storms make me anxious; I was surrounded by vicious animals and evil pigeons.

Stuck at the top of the tree, I saw two wolverines below me. I fell, running to my home, watching psychotic bats flying through burned houses. My house was in flames. I bumped over a roadblock sign and the park's entrance was infested with ferocious red-eyed rats chewing the trees and eating people's remains. On both sides, wild beasts were storming through a neighbourhood and squirrels were being eaten by vicious bats; wolverines attacked my neighbours; and I witnessed Mother Nature tearing rooftops off with an unstoppable force. Nowhere else to run, I was trapped!

This setting made me want to commit suicide. In the distance, I heard a far scream from one of my close friend from junior high, Patricia. I skipped a fence, rushing toward Patricia's house, and I tripped over a rifle, watching her chased by a stampeding creature, and I sprinted to her rescue. I took the rifle, shooting the monster as blood splattered my face.

Patricia and I walked four miles in heavy rain hearing no sounds of people. We were both trapped in this harsh reality, the end of nature. Another mile along, we looked at an old bush burned by a lightning strike; above us, we saw our neighbours' skulls hanging on wooden branches. We ran along the trail path near a creek in the middle of nowhere. It was late afternoon and still raining and we were desperate to find shelter. Across the park, Patricia and I noticed a broken green bench bitten by wolverines. Here, we shivered with no umbrella, waiting for help.

In someone's backpack lying on the ground covered in mud, we found a cell phone and a pair of car keys! I clicked the fob, and we followed the auto alarm toward a two-door military jeep just as an avalanche slid beyond the hillside. The speedometer was blinking red as I pressed the gas in acceleration. With poor visibility, seeing a wall of snow headed straight for us! This looked to me a wild rollercoaster ride.

Inside the alarming winter storm with no escape and no rescue supplies; our current position was catastrophic. Trapped in our unworking jeep, we were being dragged over a cliff by the powerful snowslide, falling in midair! From above, we spotted a bright light somewhere on the ground—a place in flames, where massive military tankers were firing cannons at wild creatures. The avalanche ripped through. We jumped from the jeep, falling, and sliding on thick snow.

Unconscious. A few hours later, we woke up lying on a wagon driving through a woodland; we watched a war party from far and I thought somebody could bring us back home. Entering the village within a woodland, we saw a full camp of hunter-gatherers. Strangled in shackles. A strong guy pushed us as we walked through a cemetery, seeing dead animals speared with arrows as blood spread across the landscape. A spiritual man approached us dressed in white silk and holding a rod. The entire camp silenced.

The spiritual man said, "Who are you?"

Patricia and I responded, "We were in a plane crash and deserted."

A warrior shouted in anger, "Kill them! They are outlaws!"

Patricia shouted, "We are from a town cursed by the alien invasion. Your tribesman brought us. We come in peace to warn you you're in danger of climate apocalypse against humanity. Around you, these lost animals led your people to famine!"

The angry spiritual man said, "Ok! For heaven's sake, you may stay at our camp for a few days and be our hunters. If you escape, you are both dead!"

Patricia's talk with the spiritual man gave us a chance to escape by morning. We were young hunters encamped and starving, fighting for survival with our hunting gear. Asleep, dreaming of a large forest, seeing a few wild animals and a snowy trail covered with toboggan tracks and footprints, as if a pack of sled dogs passed.

As we continued our long journey on the same trail, we found ourselves lost in the unusual danger of being hunted. Approaching a steep hill, we caught a bloodthirsty grizzly bear eating dead body remains with his sharp teeth—a full mouth of blood dripped on snow. We hid next to a tree, seeing the wild creature from a short distance, then we went close with our rifles.

I saw through the binoculars Patricia's slow movements six metres away from me as I camouflaged myself beside a bush. My heart pounded fast when Patricia positioned herself in an attack, keeping her gun at a straight angle to pull the trigger. A miss! The creature charged Patricia in rampage. I rushed over, pushing her aside and I took my gun, aiming at the creature, killing it with a clean shot. A nightmare—I woke up yelling, sweating. I glanced at my wristwatch and was 2:00 am.

Patricia whispered, "Andy, we should plan on making our escape before sunrise."

I said, "Good idea!"

We grabbed our hunting gear, and I kicked the door wide open. We headed north with our flashlight. It was dark and creepy hearing the howling wolves and owl sounds mimicking in the distance. I pointed my flashlight at an abandoned snowmobile beside a Christmas tree buried under heavy snow, and I found the keys on the seat post. I tried starting the engine a few times and the fifth try worked! We took off, heading north with nothing to feed ourselves.

Patricia questioned, "Andy, will they find us?"

I explained, "We are heading for a long cross-country trip outside indigenous territory. They cannot track us."

Remembering our trouble back at the camp, I had a strange thought someone might follow us using the snowmobile's tracks. It was less than a half hour till dawn and we didn't know our whereabouts with no compass and no map. Above, the night skies turned blue-orange as sunrise shed vast light throughout the forest. In the daylight, no sign of any outpost.

I recognized a town north of the highway and, to my right, an abandoned colonial-style hotel. We made a stopover, leaving our snowmobile beside the front gate, seeing rotten walls, dead pigeons, and shattered windows. We both stayed in hiding from our enemies and awaited a miracle. Dropping our bags on the floor, we both unpacked.

Patricia, in tears, said, "Andy, will we find food? Can we survive on our own?"

I hugged Patricia. "Don't worry, we will be fine working together to stay strong and hope for the best."

Our stomachs grumbled. Hungry for a good, wholesome meal before evening, we took our hunting gear and headed straight through an empty park. Less than a kilometre away, we smelled fresh bread. Reaching the factory with a thundercloud above, we approached the open gate. A robot baker—Patricia and I nodded, reminded of post-apocalypse societies entrenched in artificial science and technologies. I found a bread loaf left on the kitchen counter and we grasped it.

The alarm rang and we saw robots raging; we ran, shattering the front window. Running through the park, the storm clouds behind us, we heard thunder as large droplets fell on our heads. I looked back. The robots were chasing us.

Patricia yelled, "Faster, faster!!"

It turned nasty. We made it back to the hotel, shutting the gate and locking the doors and windows. Inside, we ate our bread. A few minutes later, the robots drilled the front gate and it slammed on the foyer floor, and we ran outside. I tried starting the snowmobile, but its unworking engine has lost fuel. We're left with no choice.

Running in the pouring rainstorm, we spotted a town. I imagined this was the place to find a safe house away from those runaway robots. Moving into the shabby village, we looked up at an entrance sign: "WELCOME TO THE VILLAGE OF BOT ROAD." No people! The world had become an uncivilized setting of despondency. This village had no road or curbed sidewalks. Our shoes leaked and socks were wet from heavy rainfall and thick mud. From behind, a dozen angry robots fired lasers and struck a restaurant in flames! We ran to an abandoned gas station, spotting a firetruck from the early seventies.

I yelled, "Hurry! Go inside, Patricia!"

Grabbing a high calibre machine rifle, I came out firing at these raging robots, hoping to not run out of shots. Patricia tried to turn on the unworking engine. We were both in serious trouble! I pulled the trigger but the machine rifle had no rounds left. I didn't know what to do next to protect her and save myself. Most shocking, a robot fired a shot which hit the fuel drum, which blasted, sweeping the entire village under heavy mud in ashes and metal debris. I rushed, and Patricia bled! I wrapped her arms around my back, walked in tears, looking elsewhere to bury her. Close to the village, I spotted a cemetery and dug a hole for Patricia's body in the rain. A last goodbye. I was on my own now.

Witnessing Earth's deterioration with no food, I walked through a degraded vineyard with burned ash and wild horses. I had a prickly sensation in my fingers after touching the sharp thorns and wondered if these might be alien organisms from another planet.

Sitting next to a tree, facing the hillside ruptured from an earthquake, I turned around and glimpsed something unusual. A red apple fell on my head, and above me, dead human bodies hanging on a cactus. Shock and dreadful fear made me leap over a stallion riding away to escape the horrors of entrenchment. I ran in fury, looking at three horses—one dark-coloured, from a racetrack competition.

I had a long and difficult ride ahead to my hometown to end this ugly fiction. Nothing would stop me! I sat on the saddle and watched the sunlight grazing in front of me, behind a rain cloud. I realized the sunlight was my compass out of this empty world, and the moon was my resting point to sleep and await the next journey.

After miles of riding, I saw through heavy smoke. I had vertigo and imagined I'd been left behind as a dying soldier within a scorching desert with no food and no water. Patricia, not with me anymore. I noticed a trail of deceased human bodies lying on rough sand after a destructive war. Dead animals everywhere. My stallion took me to a place deserted. I fainted. Waking up, lying unconscious and covered in dirt, I stood up.

On my stallion, I continued my journey, heading towards a steep hill and through a deforested land. On the distant horizon, I saw, for the first fascinating moment in my entire life, the French Alps looking as gorgeous. On top of a cliff, facing the mountain, I saw the bright sunset behind the mountains and I fell off my stallion. A few hours later, I stared at the full moon as stars glittered in the living skies above me. The stallion was my companion.

A dream became an awakening incident—I glimpsed in shock hunters running from the bushes in every corner, arrowing at my stallion. In tears, it died, and I felt heartbroken. Something hit me from behind and I fainted on the spot. I woke up unconscious in daylight and I could not move. The physical tightness of my legs squeezed by thick ropes made me hyperventilate. Inhaling the brisk-cool mountain air deep inside my lungs, I lay naked on icy rocks, subjected to torture.

In front of me, the fierce enemy carried their spears. As they approached me, I noticed a military helicopter firing in close range, shooting with unstoppable force, and I felt relieved. I was no longer a prisoner. The soldiers with machine gun came, to my relief, and they took me to the chopper alive, safe and sound!

"I am David, the commander of the Rescue Response Unit. Charmed to meet you," the co-pilot announced.

"I am Andy from Moosetown."

David replied, "Are you hurt?"

I responded in pain, "I have deep bruises on me. David, do you have a first aid kit to patch my injuries?"

"Yes, Brian, please help Andy with this—"

A while later, David announced, "Andy, we are routing to Moosetown!"

I was glad to be taken back home after this tough trip. A thousand feet above, the helicopter crosses over Lake Elizabeth where dolphins jump over wavy waters. I had no camera to take exquisite photos. Blue skies made it a glorious morning. I daydreamed, remembering those moments of having survived in the wilderness with no food and how I protected Patricia from danger.

David woke me. "We are descending into Moosetown in five minutes."

Through the window, I saw two flying saucers invading Moosetown and I fired at both. We were in real danger, and this was not the time for practicing rounds like in a video game. I watched David defending his unit from the intensity of flying saucers while the lasers made holes through the helicopter. Suddenly, the helicopter descended rapidly into a crash! I saw David's colleagues seriously injured. David and I were fighting for our lives. The last soldier to prove his bravery would be this one.

Fearing my life would end, I couldn't imagine the dangers of attacking with an empty machine gun and no other weapons. Out of bullets, I had nothing else to defend myself with except a rocket launcher to fire a shot! This was my last chance to bring violence to an end; should I die trying to save David, or risk jumping off the chopper at five hundred feet? One flying saucer kept on firing at us, and I had the rocket launcher in my hands ready to aim and pull the trigger. With precision, I shot at the flying saucer, which burst into flames!

A parachute from the compartment fell on my bare feet! David was alive. I grabbed his arms and tied the rope tightly around our waists. We dropped from the helicopter and I released the parachute in midair, falling fast, seeing a military base and soldiers below me. Breathtaking. We landed safely with minor injuries. I sat on the runway. Paramedics carried David into the ambulance.

The ambulance left, and I ran my best to catch it. Right on time, paramedics pulled me in where I could see David breathing through a ventilator. I sat beside him, worried.

I asked the paramedic, "Will David make it alive?"

Jacob responded with confidence, "Yes. Do not worry, David will be all right."

I remained silent for the long ride to the hospital. An hour passed, and we made it, stopping in front of the emergency room doors. Pulling David out of the ambulance, I went with paramedics to the emergency room. Behind me, three surgeons rushed, pushing me aside.

I asked, "Can I come?"

A nurse advised me. "No. Andy, please sit here and make yourself comfortable. Everything is going to be okay. Do you want coffee, tea?"

"Coffee," I requested.

I sat in the waiting room, patient, drinking my beverage for an hour, and no one came. The hallway was empty. I fell asleep while sitting. An hour later, the nurse woke me and I came to the emergency room. Through the window, I saw David lying on the hospital bed not breathing! Is he dead? I panicked. Another nurse entered the room, and introduced himself as Bradley Stevenson.

Bradley showed me David's medical results. "Your friend David suffered a heart attack. I am sorry, he did not make it." Bradley hugged me in condolence.

I left the hospital, sobbing, walking through the main lobby, out the front doors, upset at having no home or friend's place to protect myself from danger. My challenge is not complete. While strolling along the dark street beside an empty bus stop, I wondered, Are my neighbours still alive? Good question. I sat on the bench, trying to remember where I lived. No idea. In memory of Patricia, would I find someone like her to trust?

From a kilometre away, a transit bus approached, lightening the shadowy street. This was my chance! I remembered I lived at 78 Ridgewood Lane; someone named this street after the passing of Bill Ridgewood, the mayor of Moosetown.

Stepping inside a fifty-year-old GMC bus, I asked, "Do you know where 78 Ridgewood Lane is?"

The driver answered, "This route will take you there."

I sat on an old-fashioned green bench. An uncomfortable and noisy ride; a unique experience, different than being on a new school bus. After a half hour, the driver announced, "Ridgewood Lane," and I pulled the yellow bell cord to request my stop.

Walking with precaution along Ridgewood Lane, I found a burned car in someone's driveway. I recognized it as the bungalow of Mr. Sanderson, one of my closest neighbours. I knocked at the wooden door and it opened! Inside, I shouted, "Is anyone home?!" No answer. Not leaving, I risked my life to look everywhere for Mr. and Mrs. Sanderson. I started by searching in the living room; the sofa was flipped over, a dozen magazines lay on the carpet beside broken chairs; blood stained the white walls in the kitchen! Finding the one bedroom, I saw the most terrifying sight: my two neighbours' skeletal remains lying on the bed disgustingly! I ran out the doors screaming.

I was the last person standing. I heard no one, saw burned houses in the daylight. I found a toy bunny under a broken baby crib. Picked it up, feeling depressed, realizing this neighbourhood was no longer an active place for socialization.

Holding this cute toy in my filthy hands, I went searching for my home as a brave man in no condition to fight. Strolling along the damaged sidewalk, I saw in front of me no houses and no surrounding trees—destruction is everywhere! The brick I stood on was my destroyed house, my family under the deep pile of rubble.

Chapter 6

The Atlantic Ocean Meteorite: The Big Angel

On the late afternoon of **April 11, 1912**, Daniel Morgenson is in a Ford T Model with his family; Daniel's driver honks the car's horn while driving through the busy crowd. Sees through his right window more than a hundred suitcases scattered across the pier as people board the *Big Angel*. Daniel orders the driver to stop beside a meat shop and takes his family to sit inside a small café for the last time. He has one girl, Catherine, and one boy, Billy.

Daniel's family sits beside the window. Catherine and Billy both see the *Big Angel*, wishing to board it someday. Daniel brings coffee for his wife, Emily, and an espresso for himself. They sit as one big happy family, enjoying their last moments with Daniel before his leave. It's difficult for Emily and Billy to watch their father leaving them behind in Queenstown; they hope to meet him again soon. Will this happen?

After finishing their hot beverages, they leave the café and head straight for the dock. Walks through the crowds, Daniel hears a man announcing, "The ship will leave Queenstown in ten minutes!" The family approaches the main dock, beside the ship ladder, and Daniel says goodbye.

Daniel speaks with Catherine and Billy: "Both of you will be with your mother till I return." He kisses their cheeks and hugs them.

Emily says, "Take care of yourself and have a safe journey."

Daniel turns back. "I love you." He ascends the stairs.

After reaching for his boarding pass, Daniel approaches a deck steward and shows him it. Daniel is through and goes inside, finding his third-class cabin. He looks around at a few hundred people aboard the *Big Angel*. He's never been on a pirate ship before—though this ship has been restored as a passenger vessel. Twenty minutes later, Daniel finds his cabin—an old-style room, dark brown, constructed from wood—and meets a few nice people as his roommates. They introduce themselves: Ronald, Sean, John, and Ralph.

After settling themselves, they go fast to the top deck, knowing the *Big Angel* will leave soon. The ship moves fast! Below, people look small and Daniel sees his family and waves. "I will miss you!" The *Big Angel* gains full speed, its first time setting sail in the Atlantic Ocean.

Daniel and his friends stay on deck the whole afternoon till evening, looking at the spectacular view of the ocean and stars glowing beyond, in the far distance. The weather is cool and dark. After a long day, they go to their cabin. Daniel does not sleep, missing his family.

April 12, 1912. Daniel wakes up at 7:30 am and goes on the main deck to breathe the ocean breeze where he sees the sun reflecting on the deep blue sea. Moments later, a kid approaches Daniel, asking for help.

The boy cries, "I lost my father and cannot find him."

Daniel hugs the boy in comfort. "Don't cry. Let's go find your daddy. How does your father look?"

The boy introduces himself. "My name is Robert. He is in a dark wool suit and wears a Western-style hat." Daniel holds Robert's left hand tight, goes through the corridors.

Robert's father shouts at Daniel, "Stay away from my son! You come near him again, I will make you uncomfortable!" A threat. Daniel pays no attention.

Returns to his cabin, sad-looking. Sean asks him, "What's the matter?"

Daniel answers, "Nothing. I will not sleep this night. Maybe we should hangout?"

"Yes, Daniel, why not," Sean settles.

Daniel and the others prepare themselves for this evening's third-class party at 8:00 pm. A few hours later, Daniel's friends Sean, Ronald, John, and Ralph, are leaving with him to the party room for the celebrations. They make it before the doors close. Inside, people dance, enjoying the fun; Daniel looks at families spending time with their children while he encounters a moment of loneliness. His friends are socializing with young girls drinking beer at the tables; if Daniel's family were here, everything would be different. He drinks his whiskey; at last, an Irish girl in her mid-thirties invites Daniel to dance. A smile on his face. After the dance, she feels attracted to Daniel. They both sit chatting together.

Daniel asks, "What is your name?"

She introduces herself, "Lucy."

Daniel acquaints, "Is a pleasure to meet you."

Lucy questions Daniel, "Are you married?" Daniel excuses himself.

Daniel leaves the party, knowing that he is married, and drinks a full jug of strong beer. This is Daniel's second night aboard the *Big Angel*. He sleeps not in his cabin tonight, but outside, lying on the bench where he looks at the northern lights and star clusters while smoking his cigarette. No one here. Passed midnight, Daniel feels no wind and hears the sounds of the open sea. He has not eaten since yesterday, except for a beer drank on an empty stomach.

The next morning, **April 13, 1912**, Lucy finds Daniel sleeping on the bench in his dark leather suit and wakes him. He looks around in double-vision, drunk, and sees her. Lucy takes Daniel to her room to rest.

She knocks at the door. "Mom, dad, my friend, Daniel. Can he go with us for breakfast?"

Lucy's mother says, "Sure."

Well rested, ready to eat something, Daniel experiences being rich from poor with different choices of fresh foods and others dressed in their fine clothing. Daniel sits beside Lucy's parents and does not know how to eat as an aristocrat. Daniel enjoys eating his wholesome breakfast and says no word. Afterwards, Lucy leaves with Daniel for a stroll on deck, as they discuss the differences between them, becoming acquainted with each other the whole day. Lucy invites Daniel again for dinner that night, as she's attracted to him.

At 9:00 pm, Lucy comes out in her exquisite dress and approaches Daniel from the back. He turns around and looks at her, stunned, when she wraps her left arm around Daniel's right arm. They dance together on this romantic occasion and Lucy kisses Daniel. She is in love with him. After the dance, Daniel heads back to his cabin tired, and falls fast asleep.

April 14, 1912. Daniel sleeps till late morning and wakes up at 10:00 am, seeing his friends are gone. Cruising on the Atlantic Coast, cloudy and windy, and Daniel goes out for a smoke. Many walk and there's no sign of Lucy anywhere. Daniel goes around looking for her. Out of nowhere, Daniel hears a sonic boom and the sky turns dark as nightfall—everyone sees the meteorite falling from the thundery sky four kilometres away and it hits the Atlantic!

A plume of water vapour creates a giant water sprout, looking like a nuclear explosion has happened. Crabs fall from the fireball sky as rain, hurting everyone. This is the beginning. Daniel runs everywhere to look for Lucy; no sign of her. He suspects smoke coming from the other end of the ship, where the boiler room is, and approaches, seeing people running for their lives onto the main deck. Follows them. Outside, disaster is happening! The *Big Angel* rocks like a paper toy on the verge of being sucked in by this massive water sprout.

It forms into a tornado as ice crystals spin in the air, falling from the sky as large hail, turning into heavy rain, destroying the deck. Daniel sees up ahead that the *Big Angel* is heading in a deadly direction. It is too late to abandon the ship! Gigantic waves destroy the *Big Angel*; when it splits apart, people fall into the burning water. Daniel tries to hang onto the handrails, where he sees many survivors who cannot hold on fall to their death into the wavy ocean. Fifty have perished and a dozen of innocent children have lost their close relatives. Beside Daniel, Lucy's mother hangs on with her left arm and he tries to grab her right arm and holds tight, but he cannot handle her body weight. She falls, hitting the white sails! Daniel cries as the *Big Angel* sinks!

Daniel is the last survivor aboard this ship. Without a life jacket, he fears plunging to his death. His weak hand slips, and Daniel cannot hold on. The bowsprit collapses, tearing off the *Big Angel's* bow! Daniel looks back and sees the biggest wave ever, the height of two tsunamis! Panics. A massive wall of water with powerful currents covers Daniel and smashes through the wooden walls as the ship splits in two, sinking into the Atlantic Ocean! It detaches and Daniel is the last one who goes with it! The ship explodes into the ocean's depths. No survivors.

A week later, Emily receives a letter from the US Embassy. Everyone aboard died. A tragic day for her to read this sad letter. It is the winter of April 1912. Emily attends the funeral with her children in Queenstown, the burial of victims.

Chapter 7

A Family Vacation in Terror

We travelled across Canada as a family, taking magnificent pictures of wild animals, finding every moment exciting. At the Calgary Stampede, we spent the most time together. We visited the Fairmont Chateau of Lake Louise to breathe fresh air and see spectacular, enormous mountains. The clean water showed a bright reflection of the living skies. Living in Calgary, we paid visits to recreational parks to be up-close with nature. But I have never been to the Oldman River Dam.

So when, at school, my class was assigned a project on spatial landscapes, I convince my parents to give them an exciting opportunity to watch wildlife. After finishing my meal, I sat on the sofa.

A meanwhile later, I heard my mother's voice. "Max, dessert is ready!"

"I am sitting in the living room," I responded. My parents came downstairs.

I spoke, "My class teacher gave me an assignment to conduct a research study at Oldman River Dam in southwestern Alberta. Are we going or not?"

They both settled. "Sure, son. When do you prefer to leave?"

"Will Saturday work?"

My father said, "Ok, let's do it!"

After this talk, I was proud of myself for convincing Mom and Dad for the first time in my adolescence.

On the day of our trip, I woke up at 7:00 am, packed my belongings, and went downstairs to have breakfast. Thirty minutes later, we drove through our neighbourhood, heading for the Oldman River Dam. Ahead, we saw green traffic lights and the major sign displaying "Trans-Canada Highway."

Mom looked at the map of Alberta. "Let's head South on the 22nd through Okotoks."

Dad turned on the GPS, seeing 250 kilometers, a few hours of riding. We passed cropland where farmers fed their cattle and horses galloped across the landscape. No chance to take pictures as every minute was accounted for in our plan to reach Oldman River Dam and avoid a traffic jam.

On the interstate for three long hours with no break, I drank an apple juice on an empty stomach, exhausted. I slept for an hour. I woke up and noticed out my left window the sky darkening pitch black and strong wind gusts; from the rear, a funnel cloud was forming, turning into a deadly EF5 tornado in a matter of a few seconds!

"Mom! Dad! Behind us!" I panicked.

Nowhere to seek shelter. Speed-driving through the prairies worried about being stopped by the police, locking the doors, too late for an escape. The tornado sucked us into midair, storm clouds spun and the winds howled as two freight trains passed.

Trapped, we spun with no control, and the car windows shatter from the large hail, frequent lightning bolts, and torrential downpours. A veritable nightmare! With zero visibility, I had no idea of our physical whereabouts. We were in Tornado Alley! Inside the car, we dropped fast in midair—more shocking than being on a rollercoaster ride. We attempted a dangerous life risk to jump five hundred feet below to save ourselves before death! We shared hands as we were in this together. Holding ourselves in a tuck position, we landed flat on our backs, hitting the ground in agony. Four hundred metres away, an explosion; through the blazes, the EF5 tornado continued to rip the prairies, leaving its trail of destruction.

Storm clouds cleared. Devastation was at every corner; fallen trees lay scattered beside dead cattle, which left a trail of spilled blood along the destroyed lands. We stood in shock. We walked, finding our way back to the highway. With no car and no rescue supplies, we were at a disastrous ending. No point in arguing. Our trip to Oldman River Dam was under question.

My parents yelled at me, "Why you brought us here to be stranded?!"

I spoke with confidence, "I understand this journey has cost us much trouble. I am positive we will make it if you allow me to be your guide person, if we stick together as a family."

Mom and Dad both apologized. "Yes. Sorry, son, we overreacted." We hugged each other.

I thanked them for supporting me. It looked the storm had hit ten kilometres south. Following the tornado's aftermath, we walked on uneven prairie grounds through dust and smoke of the wreckage—tough to see the devastating impact of what Mother Nature had done to our world. We feared climate change would kill us and be tough on our survival. I was the one responsible for my parents' lives as I determined the safest direction.

Uncertainty overwhelmed me. I did my best to safeguard my parents from perishing. We walked on the grassland, shocked to find no food, grain resources destroyed and dead cattle from the tornado's devastating impact. I could not afford to make wrong guesses and our lives depended on me guiding my parents towards a straight path to the mainland. In the meantime, we had to stay strong together.

Suffering from thirst, I didn't know how long we'd been under no sun and cloudy skies as we walked in pain. Around me, the marshes were ruined after the storm, and dry soil complicated our survival, as natural resources were facing degradation in this dangerous climate, putting our lives at risk.

Seeing the devastated landscape was a terrible moment of great despair as tears filled my eyes. We wandered further, finding the nearest highway across a degraded landscape hit hard by the tornado's aftermath. It had been a tough day. Mom and Dad needed to rest; I had to keep a close watch on my surroundings. No harm would come to them.

I spent days reflecting on the challenges and the dangers which we might face at any stage throughout this journey. Each day, I presented my own views to persuade my parents to consider correct choices, which would keep us safe until we could reach Oldman River Dam. There's an old saying: a shepherd guides its flock in the same direction; an important responsibility to figure out life-saving opportunities. I have the guts to bring Mom and Dad through hostile areas, and I will not risk leaving them!

A week had passed since the storm. We had walked 30 kilometres with no map. We continued to walk in daylight.

I announced, "Good news! According to the winds, we are closer to the interstate."

My parents were glad to hear this. With a surprise, I noticed a long road close by. We jumped into laughter. I never thought this moment would come! This journey was not over yet. I knew heading to Oldman River Dam on the roadway by foot was risky.

We saw no cars and no buses. We sat on the ground exhausted from these long miles of walking. Mom and Dad lay on the road, dehydrated with no drinking water. A nightmare! Fighting for survival with no resources and nowhere to seek shelter, we faced the hardest challenge in our lives. I was the one remaining to take care for my parents.

I could not watch my parents in a coma—I stood, and my heartbeat pounded fast. Food, water, and trees were gone. I knew Planet Earth would turn into a desert—too dangerous and living matter on the verge of extinction.

There was no chance for survival. My parents' lives concerned me as I considered leaving them behind in search of water. Should I search for something to feed empty mouths, or wait till a vehicle approaches? These questions gave me a headache. I had a hard time thinking of other ways to protect them.

No space to think. I left them behind and run to search for food and water. In tears, I went quickly, picking up my pace, running through a dark tunnel—a risk to save Mom and Dad before it was too late. I jumped over many abandoned cars buried deep under the sand, noticing rat colonies biting human skulls. I escaped from this freakish place, hoping to find resources. I looked to my left and saw Oldman River Dam! A coincidence.

I stood on top of a cliff with no idea how I would make it alone. Scared to descend along slippery rocks, I took the time to think of safer ways to avoid shortcuts, and to do everything to keep my parents alive, no matter the trouble. I was ready to face the unexpected challenges on my own.

I had no energy to run, worried whether my parents were both alive. My leg stiffness made it more difficult for me to walk long distances. I should have brought with me a few rescue supplies.

In front of me, I saw a roadblock, a cliff to my right, a reservoir full of water kilometres away, and a tall and massive tree close by. I didn't know if this life-saving moment would happen—meanwhile, I prayed by thanking God for guiding me.

I walked over steep rocks towards the reservoir. No water! I found an empty bucket lying on dirt. I had to risk injury for my parents' sakes. We would continue the rest of our short journey to the Oldman River Dam.

I looked around, and there was a coconut tree in the far corner. Running towards it, I climbed the branches which prevented me from falling over, and I grasped with both palms, hanging like a gymnast. I found two coconuts and shook the branch a dozen times and they hit the dirt. I managed with my physical strength and outstanding balance. Grabbing both coconuts, filling those with fresh water, I carried each one in separate palms, walking over big rocks. Heading straight towards the tunnel for another kilometre, I jogged with added weight on me. After twenty minutes of speed-walking, in front of me was a bright light.

Outside the tunnel, I noticed Mom and Dad lying flat on the ground and I rushed, splattering water on their burnt faces, and they did not wake. I open their mouths, giving them more water in intervals, but still their consciousness was unrecoverable! I tried doing CPR, and no heartbeat! Terrible news for me. I cried on the spot, hugging them both in tears, never seeing them again.

Asking myself, how will I carry both their bodies from this place? From a distance, someone was driving a Vespa scooter towards me. I waved my arms high. Moments later, a girl on the scooter stopped beside me, taking off her helmet.

I wept. "Can you help me? My parents are deceased and I need a ride."

She responded, "Sure, no worries. I am sorry for your loss. My name is Jennifer, and what is yours?"

I responded, "Thank you for your condolences. I am Max."

Jennifer helped me carry my parents' bodies, and I sat on the rear seat holding tight. Sitting on the scooter felt more fun than riding inside a car.

I advised, "Follow through the tunnel and to your far right, there's a reservoir beside a tall coconut tree. To warn you, a sandy trail is up ahead filled with rocks."

"Ok," Jennifer replied.

I knew my trip to Oldman River Dam was over, but most important, I should pay my respects in silent prayer. The sad moment came when Jennifer helped me bury my parents' bodies.

I stood, praying, "Please, forgive me."

Jennifer spoke from her heart. "Max, will you take me home to be your close friend?"

I said, "Yes, I will! Are you coming to live with me?"

"Why not?" She smiled.

Jennifer tells me, "I am from Texas, alone with no family, and riding on a scooter to find a new home."

We started the scooter and started travel back to Calgary—a happy ending! This time, I was not alone. It was tough on me, leaving this place to start a new life with Jennifer, but we had a quest together.

We travelled alone in favourable weather until unexpected rain hit late afternoon. Jennifer was an expert rider, handling the scooter well for her age. This was the first time I'd enjoyed cruising at top speed.

The setting looked familiar to when my parents and I wandered across the landscape in the tornado's aftermath. I could still see the storm damages. We were in the dead zone of Tornado Alley. I kept this in secret, not alarming her, hoping we would make it through with our luck. Sitting on the pillion, I paid close attention to what was behind us, the ruins of widespread devastation surrounding us. I breathed through dusty air while cruising on the fast scooter with no glasses and no helmet.

My ass hurt from riding long hours of road in the middle of nowhere. We'd covered over a hundred kilometres through gusty weather. We passed the destruction, heading towards the interstate leading us into Calgary. I feared we might be in danger, if we ran out of fuel.

Exhausted, I stayed awake. Less than a kilometre away, a major highway appeared in front of us and a big city behind a tall tower!

I cheered, "Calgary, my home! We made it!" I tapped Jennifer's right shoulder.

Headed for downtown, we followed the exit sign, approaching the major intersection. Near my home, I gave Jennifer directions. She made a left turn, heading straight towards a small neighbourhood, my house on the right side. Our last stop!

I said, "Jennifer, welcome home!" I found the keys in my pocket.

Opening the door, Jennifer grasped my hand, scared we were in a stranger's home. Inside, nothing had changed and my home looked the same. We went through the kitchen, upstairs to my bedroom; everything was tidy and clean, except for my homework lying on the floor beside my study desk. I showed Jennifer my room.

Jennifer commented, "Max, nice place you have! Will we sleep in the same room?"

I spoke to her, "We are still best friends. Don't worry, my house is safe where we will spend the best times together. Trust me."

Turning on the television in my room, Jennifer and I watched a comedy show. Hours passed in laughter as we had a great time. On late Monday evening, we were both hungry and wanted to make dinner before sleep. Jennifer took a quick shower and I went to the kitchen to prepare something special for our first date.

Still plenty of leftover foods in the refrigerator, lucky us! I found a chocolate cake cut in half, turkey slices wrapped in aluminum foil, and a cheese platter with a bowl of salad. I put the items on the kitchen counter while turning on the oven. I prepared the salad. I heard Jennifer's voice from behind, was stunned to see her dressed in a tricolour skirt. She sat on a chair beside the dinner table, stared at me in glamour. I turned back and there was no food on the kitchen counter!

Angry at myself, I said, "Damn it! The food is gone!"

"Calm yourself, Max," Jennifer said.

I stormed around the house searching for the culprit! I looked everywhere, through shelves and under the furniture, and suddenly, I heard unusual sounds coming from the attic. I pulled the attic ladder and saw a goblin hiding behind the stack of boxes eating the rest of our food!

I burst into anger. "Who are you? What are you doing here?"

The evil goblin looked at me with his green eyes, ready to attack me! With nothing to defend myself, I ran downstairs panicking as it chased me. Help! Jennifer came to my rescue and chased the goblin. I rushed to the window, saw her fist-fighting the goblin on the lawn where it ran away through other homes stealing neighbours' food. She saved my life; someday, I would make it up to her. I was feeling awful our first night together had come to a shameful ending!

Later, Jennifer came inside through the front doors in her messy look. I was afraid she would kill me. Jennifer approached me in humour as she had won her fight against the goblin! Jennifer and I were both brave. It was not the end of our evening. We sat together on the floor on a romantic occasion, celebrating our first date and victory.

Chapter 8

The Farm

Delivered into the dreamworld in 1990, living on a colonial-style farm, I was brought-up to learn cultivation practices, and take care of the farm. I carried many of my household pets.

A few years later, I am six. One of my early duties is watering tomatoes and herbs during the hot summer. I gain many responsibilities to be completed by the end of each workday and I enjoy working outdoors.

I will never forget when I planted my first tomato seed. My mother will be proud of me if I conduct an experiment on plants. This unveils me as being an environmentalist. I feel the smell of a home-cooked meal baking from downstairs; the aromas make me hungry!

I ask Mom at the dinner table, "Are we returning to the garden?"

Mom replies, "Sure, Zack. We will head out after you finish eating."

Again, I will see if my tomato seed has grown. It grows tall as I stare at the cherry tomatoes hanging on branches. I know deep in my heart I might become a gardener someday, having my farm.

When I am a teenager, my parents motivate me to be a farmer and teach me to preserve the ecosystem by feeding the cattle, planting seedlings, and collecting the grain for harvest.

Becoming older, I spend most of the time working in the fields, cultivating fresh fruits. We grow many kinds of vegetables on our home soil.

It took strength to build the farm, where we connect our farming spirits with nature. In the countryside, we preserved plants with ideas to improve biodiversity.

A Brave Survivor's Striking Story

One morning, I leave home for school in my ridiculous farmer's outfit, strolling along the prairies, a city in front of me. I hear my mother's voice in the wind; I look back, seeing the dust clouds darken. I am trapped amid this alarming setting as my parents' lives are in danger. A sandstorm might wipe out the farm.

Flames make me thirsty while I roam in sweltering weather. Stuck between both worlds, confused whether to continue my journey or head back home, I am irritated. I should have stayed with my parents rather than roaming in the middle of nowhere. It is too late for a return.

I have no supplies and I'm alone. I have no water and no meal. I am on a road less travelled where danger threatens me at every corner. Behind me, a sandstorm comes in my direction with an eminent threat, and I am worried about my parents' survival. I do not know where east will bring me.

How did the prairies turn into a North African desert? Under the red sun in an opaque sky, I wander for hours on sand filled with sharp, pointy rocks when I notice a sandstorm. No place to seek shelter; I run towards a distant flatland to hide from danger, and behind me, a wall of dust pellets blows through my ripped clothes. Rushing for cover, I am caught within this deadly setting as I duck, lying flat on my stomach; the ground shakes with the powerful winds.

A half-hour has passed and I am still stuck under thick sand, attempting to free myself from this mess, and no one is coming to my rescue. I grasp a strong underground root, which brings me up onto solid ground. Too exhausting. Searching in shock, I am in a different world. I notice the desert turning into a small town. Where will I be heading next? I will stay in this village to find supplies.

I see dunes. People wear fine clothing as if they are in Africa. Strolling within the bazaar, I see fresh foods not the same as back home, searching for something to eat, looking for water to ease my awful thirst. I find a well beside a naked kid begging for money. It saddens me to watch the cruelty of impoverishment. Our planet has changed from human impact.

I approach the kid. "What is your name?"

"Ibrahim," he responds.

I give an open hand to him for introductions. "My nickname is Zack. Can you help me find food in this village? If you save me, I will allow you to be part of my journey. Return home and live free."

"Okay," Ibrahim muffles in tears.

Near tents, impoverished people starve with no access to freshwater. I am somewhere on a different continent. Ibrahim points to a shop on wheels where an old man sells raw meat.

I speak in English. "How much is the pita?"

"Five shekels," the old man offers.

I speak, "I came here to this town with no money."

Ibrahim translates in Arabic. The old man gives me the pita for free.

I wave my arm. "Thank you."

At least I can feed myself with something. No camping supplies. I can still return home, but I have Ibrahim with me. Before we leave, he stops by to meet his friend as I wait. I see someone giving him a bow with arrows and a hunting knife. Ibrahim runs to me, believing we are ready for this long trip across the desert.

We follow the sand dunes for five kilometres north, feeling thirsty. We have pita as a quick snack before approaching the cliff. Never in my life have I tasted a good orange, not the navel ones!

"Ibrahim, no, I am much taller than you." He looks frustrated.

I have a fruit-picking experience; my mother taught me to collect the best ones. I grab my knapsack, climbing the tree to grasp the fruit until I have a full load. My knapsack is filled with oranges, and Ibrahim reaches into the sack and firmly grasps it with both hands, putting it on the ground. I open the knapsack, giving an orange to Ibrahim and one to myself. As we peel the skin from these oranges, both of our faces are splattered with syrup and the sweetness. This fruit supplies the energy to continue our journey across the desert.

Feeling a grumbling sensation, a full stomach, I need a nap. Waking up, we glance at the glowing sunset as we move forward, making a run towards the small cliff where we have a bird's-eye view of everything beyond the horizon.

Reaching the cliff, we still need more time to ascend before night-fall. Will we be able to climb with no hunting gear and no rope? Ibrahim volunteers first. He climbs with strength and outstanding balance. I never expected this boy to go up the tall cliff! Below, dust impairs my vision, forcing me to ascend! Ibrahim waves his outstretched arms, tossing me a lengthy strand from leafy branches. I reach it with a grasp. Ibrahim pulls me. The strand splits apart! I hold it with both hands, using my strength to climb the rocks, feeling the tension in my legs.

I scream, "Ibrahim, help!! I can't hold on any longer."

Ibrahim throws me a lengthy wooden branch, and I make it! Ibrahim and I look at the gorgeous sunset. We have nothing to feed ourselves but we light the campfire, looking at the magnificent view for birds to hunt. It is nightfall and we're exhausted from rock climbing. I stay up for another half-hour, seeing Ibrahim asleep. Ibrahim is a lost orphan with no family.

I wonder whether to take him as my scout, set him free, or pursue my journey alone. As a single child with no brother and no sister, I was brought up by my parents never to abandon someone. I'm too soft for betrayal. Guys with a moral sense have such generosity—I will take Ibrahim for company, not leaving him abandoned in the wilderness. We are both in this together, fighting for our survival without disturbing unwanted enemies.

In the late morning, something unusual happens. We see small birds flying; Ibrahim postured himself, taking a clean shot at one with the arrow as a feast for a wholesome breakfast. After our meal, we plan our descent from the mountain and figure out our next direction. My ability to return home is under question in the middle of this desert, where climate change overwhelms me. Staying strong is part of our adulthood and we are both prepared to take life risks to save ourselves from danger.

Behind the cliff, a narrow path connects to a long slope. Going along, we see dead bodies eaten by large colonies of blood-sucking insects; more of them crawl as we run to the light—too late! These creeping insects cover Ibrahim's entire body, and I had no choice but save my own life.

I am out of this cave, alive. A thick wall of dust blows through my face! Trapped inside the sandstorm! A few moments later, there's rubble everywhere and from tall sand caves crawling insect colonies have carried Ibrahim's remains beneath the ground, swallowed by quicksand.

The tragedy of losing Ibrahim. I walk in the shadows, trying to discover the exact direction of home as my journey continues with no companion. I am lost within the wilderness; seeing nothing breaks my heart and I have nothing to cure my stress. Saying a few last words to myself about Ibrahim, I put his hunting bow beside his resting place.

In tears, I say, "Rest in the underworld in peace. I hope we meet again."

I point my finger up, testing the wind direction. No air. Gloomy weather makes it difficult for me to decide which path I should take. I stare around where there was heavy smog; the outlands! Another hundred miles of smog with no rest stop; keeping myself safe and aware of eminent danger. I cannot afford to lose my pace.

Exhausted from dehydration, I fear returning home will be a breath-taking challenge as constant stress brings me nothing but misfortune. With no roadmap and no compass, should I follow another direction? I planned on moving west towards the ash. Running for five miles, I hear thunder rumbling from a close distance. With no umbrella, I feel torrential rain pour on my half-naked body when a lightning bolt strikes beside me. Seconds later, I suspect fire surrounding me. Trapped inside the fiery circle, my heartbeat pounds in discomfort.

My backpack is the one item I have. Inside, I find a lengthy rope which belonged to Ibrahim, and I tie it around my abdomen and I throw the strand around the cactus to pull me over the flames.

I mutter, "Zack, you can do this!" I swing, making a rough landing on solid ground, suffering in pain from the deep-cut bruises.

Tears in my eyes, I say, "Where will I find medicine!?"

I can hardly stand up with these bruises and I take small footsteps. Both of my limbs needed patching. Behind me, fire burns in the distant landscape as I continue my quest, heading west. I experience sad thoughts, feeling anguished at being lost. My parents should have taught me how to survive rather than lecturing me about growing my own vegetables. I hope Mom and Dad are still alive. Life is cruel!

In my heart, I stay strong. Experiencing double vision while seeing a rotten landscape, I faint from weakness and wake up lying on the ground in the middle of a scorched plantation. Looking around in shock, I look beyond the hillside and the plantation in flames! Scared, I experience a sudden stiffness in my spinal cord when I break through the wooden fence; I see the wreckage of my home, smell stinking dead cattle, see chicken feathers lying on dirty mud and the land pastures grazed worse than a wildfire. I am heartbroken, wondering who might have done this. Could it be a natural disaster?

In misery, I go inside the house, taking a life risk to look for my parents. I do not find them. Choking from the heavy smoke while inside the burning house, having no access to the stairwell, I pass through the living room, kicking the backdoor; I look both ways and hear a sudden scream as my mother's voice sounds from the shed.

I rush and as a group of ferocious half-human monsters leave a path of destruction along the fields. It is too late for gunfire. Inside the shed, my parents' bodies lean over a haystack, bitten by a werewolf. Carrying each one of them in my arms, I create a cemetery and make a silent funeral alone.

Fumes come out from the house where it double-splits in the drenching rain. This tough moment weakens me as a person struggling alone within an uncivilized world. Survival always depended on the fittest—myself. I pay my respects to the dead, find food, and watch for danger. Tonight, I will sleep beside my parents' graves. The sound of wolf packs howling beyond the hillside and owls mimicking spooky sounds discomfort me. Sound asleep, I dream about when I came into this world, raised on the farm.

I will take revenge on the death of my parents. I never imagined the farmland turning into a battlefield filled with dead bodies. I will fight for my survival and not surrender. Vengeance will decide for me which path I choose. My time will come. I will assign myself important duties, preparing for an ultimate disaster. "Power" is my secret to win the war and I must glorify my parents' souls in the heavens, making them proud as a brave son who can fight.

Going for a stroll, searching for wood to make weapons and set traps to capture foes, I find a water sprinkler which I will use for spraying toxic chemical fertilizers; I have Daddy's old hunting rifle hidden under a dusty wooden shelf. Beside the house, I dig a deep hole, burying excess resources. Preparations have been made.

The tractor is my last resort for an escape. My parents used to use the tractor, and I hope the motor still works. I try starting the engine several times and nothing. Checking the empty fuel containers, I make a quick run, grabbing two large gas barrels inside the garage. I fill up the motor. Turning on the engine, it works! I drive the tractor home and hide it behind the farm for an escape.

I will hide behind the haystack and watch through a binocular for approaching invaders. As I'm preparing myself for an attack, the opening and closing of my eyes preoccupies me and back pain stiffens both my arms and legs. Quiet. I starve for days, suddenly weak, as this journey puts me through chronic stress with no food.

Left alone in the brutal dark world, I fear death; my survival within dystopia concerns me while I witness terrifying monsters slash and burn homes. It is pitch-black outside; the damp foggy air makes me sweat from fear. Beyond the landscape, the yellow full moon looks spooky, and massive storm clouds build, covering the stars in the night sky. Something is going to happen. Thunder rumbles as I prepare my supplies. I'm reloading my rifle with ten bullets when I hear the approaching enemy.

Behind a horse wagon, barbarians rage towards me with heavy artillery and strong armour shields. I reach out my rifle, take a clean shot, and kill two. I grab a metal shovel, hitting one of them in the head as blood splatter on my face. Outside, a small army of barbarians runs across the farmland in the drenching rain frequented by lightning, which warns me not to leave the shed. They come; I push the buggy forward. It hits them—lying on the ground in pain.

I aim the shotgun. "Bloody hell! Why are you here? To kill me?!"

I shoot them. One left—a runoff killer with double-edged swords dressed in dark armour on a black stallion. The wild stallion gains speed with powerful force as the killer approaches me fast. I stand near the entrance in fear of death. The barbarian throws in front of me a chain of human skulls and jumps off his stallion, pointing his double-edged sword, attacks me in anger. I grab a wooden box and swing the weapon as the killer hits me in the stomach. I fall over a buggy, hitting the wall; I find a gas container and a pack of matches. I open it and spill everything over the killer's back and I flee.

Four hundred metres away, behind me, a gigantic explosion—I see the shed bursting into flames! I run back to the shed and seen nothing but dead bodies burning in the fire. It's looking like I won. I notice something strange; the storm has ended as stars shine in the night sky. I hear my parents' voices in the wind.

I should rebuild the shed from wood timbers and restore my farmland. The week following the disaster, I rebuild the shed, using the tractor to pull wood. On the seventh morning, outside, the sky turns into a dark monsoon as heavy precipitation forms. Rain droplets drip onto my face.

I react: "Thank you, God."

I come home in my wet clothes and wait till the storm ends. The rainfall lasts for five days. On the sixth morning, the rainfall stops, and the grass turns verdant! Fresh air outside in the country-side; the early morning breeze feels good after a rainy night. The sun is out and the birds chirp! I don't stay at home. It's a good idea to take a stroll.

Leaving home, I think of a great idea to expand another hectare of tomato plantation wiped out from the war. I still have not forgotten this tragic event when a werewolf killed my parents. Having lost them in the shadows, I am ashamed. I cannot put this behind me.

In the garden, the kale, mushrooms, and spinach have grown well, splendid for this evening's tasty soup! I gather everything in a basket and bring it over back home, making the ingredients in a large bowl. Ready to make the tastiest soup I ever had, I stand in the kitchen. The lamps shake! Outside, I see a cyclonic twister heading straight towards my direction. I rush to search for a hiding place. I hear my parents' voices, am discomforted by the ghosts of lost lives.

They speak to me: "Something is coming! Run away, my son!"

Through the window, I see their faces. Strong winds spin tree branches, hitting my rooftop. Doors shatter, bringing hail into my house with nature's powerful force, a dangerous motion which gives me the creeps. I wait till the storm ends.

I worry what will happen to me if I leave this place with nothing in my hands. I cannot abandon my birthplace to go on another roadless journey. No place to hide from unanticipated phenomena. I know being trapped within a strange planet of emergent dystopia, evil spirits of the hostile world, will bring vagabonds to attack me. It is better to stay and wait.

The winds die and I see sunlight in front of me; I open the closet doors and see a big mess in my room: shattered glass on the floor, fallen tree branches, and dead squirrels. The living room looks terrible. My handmade furniture and pots and pans lie damaged. Outside, it looks much worse than last week's storm. My garden is destroyed and my house is detached!

No power to renovate. I waste time doing tiresome chores and all of the hard work alone. I cannot handle this! Have not eaten my bowl of soup! A sad ending. I live in an abandoned farm in isolation until the end of my lifetime with no food.

Chapter 9

The Haunted House at Smithson Lane

Tom is tired of partying after work. Instead, to play today's lottery worth $5 million, he goes inside the convenience store on Murray Street.

He approaches the clerk and says, "I want to buy a three-dollar lottery ticket for today's raffle prize of $5 million."

The clerk responds, "Ok."

"Will the results appear on today's draw this evening?"

"Yes."

He gives the printed ticket with these numbers: 03, 15, 27, 35, 40, 48.

Tom walks on the busy sidewalk towards Grenview Subway Station. Praying, he says, "God, make me win today's lottery draw, giving my family a chance to buy a new home and move out of our apartment." He opens the doors, going through the collector booth, dropping his four-dollar fare, taking the southbound train to Madison Station at Harrison Street.

At Madison Station, Tom goes up the escalator towards the exit doors. Outside, the weather is gloomy. A rainy evening ahead. With no umbrella, he rushes along the sidewalk and the rainfall starts. Making it to 138 Harrison Street, he goes inside his apartment building. Heavy downpours and thunder rumbles while Tom ascends the stairwell. Stares at his wristwatch, and it is 5 pm—a few hours remaining before the draw.

Tom knocks, and Vince opens the door. "Daddy is home!"

It's a great idea to have a hot meal after the subway commute. In the room, undressing, Tom wonders if his luck might change, hopes his raffle numbers appear on the television before bedtime.

While eating, Tom questions his family, "Do you want to live in a vast house? Today, after work, I bought a raffle ticket for this evening's $5 million prize draw!"

They look shocked, eating their meal in silence. He's never gambled and is afraid to lose. He can't wait to hear the announcement! Waiting for the exhilarating moment in their lives, Tom is nervous if this ticket might be a loss for the family.

Tom tells Angela, "Please turn off the movie. The lottery ticket results will be in five minutes!"

He grabs his lottery ticket from his jacket, sits on the sofa watching tv, and Angela shares hands with her son.

A news journalist announces on radio, "Ray Arnold from Radio Station 125. Today's winning numbers for $5 million are: 03, 15, 27, 35, 40, 48." Tom's forehead sweats.

"We have won!" He jumps in laughter as the lottery winner of tonight's draw!

Tom mentions, "They will invite us tomorrow to be interviewed on radio and claim our winnings in a full cash load!"

The family celebrates the night as first-time lottery winners! The next morning, tired after yesterday's party without much time to make it to the radio station, they take a taxi uptown where winners claim their prizes.

Forty minutes later, they arrive at a massive thirty-floor glass building. Through the main entrance doors in the lobby, taking the elevator up to floor twenty, they see a hallway with glass floors and many gold-coloured mirrors. Forgetting which room to enter, they experience trouble finding the unit number.

Angela asks, "Are we on the right floor?"

"Yes. We will find it," Tom responds.

Vince approaches someone. "My parents and I are the lottery winners. Know which room we must go to?"

Joseph, an employee, says, "Follow me, and I will show you the way."

Accompanied by Joseph, the family looks surprised—the hallway is bigger than their apartment. After a minute of walking straight towards room 208, they see the sign "Lottery Centre." Inside, a group of photographers waits for Tom beside the door.

"Good morning and congratulations! Are you ready to have your pictures taken?"

Tom responds, "Yes, we sure are!"

They entered the photography room, and Tom comes to have his picture taken. Unfair! Angela sits with Vince on the sofa waiting for Tom. Fifteen minutes later, Tom comes out happy dancing across the office, and they all jump in joy, holding the winning ticket together as they head for the elevator. This is the most exciting day of their lives—coming home with the jackpot!

Downstairs in the lobby, a limousine driver questions them. "Your name is Howler, I presume? I have been instructed to give you a ride. After you."

Tom sits in the limousine a rich man, attracting others' attention. The driver drops the family off beside their home, and they don't have to pay for this ride—a one-time opportunity. Each helps to carry the heavy suitcase with cash upstairs to the apartment. Tiring, indeed! At home, the family sits on the sofa discussing their move, and which house they want to buy.

Vince mentions, "Which school will I be going? My friends?"

Tom points out, "You will make new friends and I will find you an elite school to become a better student to reach your educational goals. Let's celebrate!"

This will be a tough move. Tom plans to do research tonight and contact a few real estate agents tomorrow. Celebrating, Tom opens the champagne! Mom has this interesting idea to hang the winning ticket on the wall in their new home. Tomorrow will be a busy day planning the move.

The next morning, the family wakes up exhausted. Tom tells Vince to go to his last day of school and Angela will tell her boss they are moving. Tom is alone in the apartment, calling a dozen real estate agents, inquiring with them which house is for sale around $2 million. It will be difficult for Tom to consult with his family. He wants to find the best house as a big surprise!

Joe, the realtor, speaks, "I am selling a wonderful house in Dallas! Your family will love it! The house has spectacular scenery, a great camping spot, a swimming pool, and a patio! Are you interested?"

Tom says, "Yes."

Joe confirms, "The house is on Smithson Lane."

Tom responds, "I live in New York. My name is Tom Howler, and I am bringing my family with me to see the house. Could we meet on Thursday this week at noon?"

Joe confirms, "Yes, will do! Ok, bye!"

A smart decision to see this house is knowing the place fits their location. Tom will tell this exciting news to his family.

A few hours later, Tom greets them at the door. "Welcome! Did you have a good day today? I found us a new house in Dallas!"

Vince shouts, "What house?"

Tom says, "You will see. We will leave the day after tomorrow and start preparing ourselves tomorrow morning!"

A bored and a sad ending. Surprised by the looks on their faces, Tom makes it a quiet evening. Tom will have to rent a truck and load everything, making it easier for safe travel. He plans their route from New York to Dallas. It is 6 am and they wake up early, eating a quick breakfast and afterwards packing everything till late evening.

Gathering heavy supplies and wrapping the furniture with plastic bags and duct tape, the family is busy working non-stop till midnight. They finish most of the work. Tom organizes his personal items. Tom knows it will be a long trip, a full day of driving along the highway following the route to Washington, heading to Tennessee through Arkansas. He's completed most of the duties and prepared the family for tomorrow's morning departure. Before going to bed, Tom calls his manager.

George responds, "Hey, Tom, how are you doing?"

Tom answers, "Fine. Thank you. I am letting you know tomorrow I am moving to Dallas with my family. I am quitting my job as the financial representative."

George responds, "Are you sure, Tom? You always have been a fantastic worker to our company. Fine. Best of luck with your future endeavours. I hope everything goes well with your move. Please, give warm kisses from me to your family."

Tom says his last words, "I will," and drops the call.

After the phone call, Tom is too heartbroken to mention the resignation from work. Coming out of his bedroom, he finds the living room empty. It is bedtime.

The family has little sleep, troubled by this move and how will the house fit their liking? Who knows? Early the next morning, honking sounds, and Tom glances through the window, seeing a large truck.

Rushing downstairs towards the street, he hears, "Are you Tom Howler?"

"Yes, I am."

"Are you ready to bring the items?"

"Yes," Tom responds.

Tom goes back to the apartment, letting his family know to help carry the boxes from downstairs, including the furniture. The U-Haul driver, Alek, and his colleagues help. Tom is the one in charge of driving this truck on a long road, leaving the city for Dallas to guide his family through dangerous highway conditions.

On the highway, leaving New York, Vince cries over missing part of his class today and his best friends. Tom is silent as he concentrates on the road with no argument.

He's excited to make it to the house early. Hopes this will happen. He's responsible for improving his family's active lifestyle for good health, which will be a challenging task for Tom.

Tom is taking a life risk. He checks if everything is okay; Angela and Vince are both sound asleep. Tom pays close attention to his driving and watches out for highway signs, a tough task for someone who has no truck driving experience. He cruises on a narrow road, passing through Maryland, with still many hours left of travel.

Ahead, no cars, no people. A strange impression of being trapped in the middle of nowhere. In front of him, the sun's luminosity glows through the windshield, wakes his family up and makes it hard to look at the traffic signs.

Angela asks Tom, "Where are we?"

He responds, "I don't know."

Tom notices a highway sign: "Welcome to Prescott, Arkansas." Travelling along the Highway 30, making no rest stop, he's afraid of being pulled over by thieves. They drive through a small town with no houses where people live in their RVs; a different lifestyle. Prescott behind them, they continue the journey towards Dallas, another 360 kilometers, a four-hour road travel. He's tired of focusing on the road nonstop for twenty-three hours.

Turning on the headlights as it becomes darker, he sees more cars and light poles; Tom will have to drive through busy traffic and watch out for roaming animals till they make it to Dallas in two hours.

Around 8 pm, it's dark and Tom's back hurts from driving long distances with no break and no food. Ahead, lights glow in the far distance, and a huge electronic highway sign displays "Welcome to Dallas." They made it! The family screams in joy, celebrating the arrival!

Tom makes a right turn on Highway 30 to exit the freeway and parks the truck outside a large shopping mall, turns off the ignition, and falls fast asleep. He will continue driving in the morning to find the home.

The next morning, the family has a breath of fresh air before they move on to finding their dream home. Tom looks at traffic signs within the neighbourhood and at last, he sees the road sign for Smithson Lane ahead!

Tom shouts, "Look to your right!"

Vince questions, "Where is our new home?" Turn left, stopping the truck beside the street curb, Tom calls Joe—the real estate agent.

Tom argues with Joe, "You didn't tell me the location."

Joe replies, "75 Smithson Lane. I am driving in a red Mini Cooper and I will meet you in thirty minutes."

Tom responds, "I am in my orange-white truck waiting in the neighbourhood."

When Joe honks, approaching us, he shouts, "Follow me!" Tom starts the ignition, driving in the same direction; a few minutes later, they see a house across the street and a real estate sign on the lawn! They stop. The house contractors have finished renovating the house. A surprise.

Joe unlocks the front door. Tom walks around in the living room, excited. The kitchen looks exquisite, and Vince goes upstairs to see his new bedroom. Tom speaks with Joe about buying the house, knowing this place will be expensive but he wants to give up the lottery winnings for the sake of finding a new home.

Joe talks, "I can sell this house to you for no less than $2 million."

Tom replies, "I need to talk with my wife."

"Ok," Joe responds.

Strolling in the garden, they discussing their decision. Angela speaks with Tom alone. "Can we afford this house?"

This question fills his mind with complications and negative thoughts, but he makes a final decision.

"We will manage this together as a family. Trust me. Let's buy this house."

Seeing Joe sitting on the patio smoking his fine cigar, they approach, taking a seat in front of him and signing the cheque. After filling out the papers, Joe gives Tom the keys to the home! Tom looks for Vince to give good news.

Tom finds him. "This house is yours, too! We will live together for the rest of our lives."

Tom runs back to the truck, bringing the furniture over to the house. He'll need help with organizing and the finishing touches. He's hoping his handy skills can renovate this place.

Step by step, they bring everything in and stack the boxes, putting strong efforts into helping each other as an active family. Tiredness does not stop them from working hard. A few hours later, Tom comes to help Vince with organizing his room.

Tom opens the door. "Son, how are you doing? Having a good time?"

Vince responds, "I am hungry!"

Tom shouts, "Angela, do we have any food?"

She answers, "We don't have any. I will ask Joe about a nearby supermarket."

"Hi Joe, this is Angela, Tom's wife. I apologize for not introducing myself. Is there a supermarket close by? I need to buy groceries."

Joe responds, "Do you need a ride?"

Angela says, "Sure, you are too kind! First, I need to tell my husband I am going to buy food. Oh, Tom! I am leaving for the grocery store with Joe."

She's out, and Tom is alone to finish the household work and clean the garden. An hour later, Joe's car approaches. Angela comes out with a full load of shopping bags—Tom rushes over to help and thanks Joe. She bought pizza, soft drinks, apple pie, and two bags of chips. A brilliant party.

Angela announces, "Dinner will be ready in thirty minutes."

Tom sets up the tv in the living room to watch a family movie before sleep. Tom smells the aroma of fresh pizza.

Angela shouts, "Let's eat!"

Tom speaks, "Before we eat our delicious homemade meal, I want to say grace:

> *Dear God, thank you for bringing us the money to buy our home;*
>
> *The family is going to be different;*
>
> *I praise the heavenly Lord to bless on this day of health, wealth, happiness. Amen."*

The family eats dinner at the table. The environment looks different than the old apartment in the suburbs—no sounds of busy cars and no disturbing neighbours. After the meal, Vince turns on the television, putting on a family movie. They watch the film, having apple pie for dessert and are tired from today's intensive work. Much more needs to be done. They turn off the television before bedtime.

In the middle of the night, Tom hears Vince screaming from his room—runs upstairs, seeing him turning into a white-haired, evil old man. Blood vomits from his mouth—Tom carries Vince's body in his arms. Food poisoning? Tom suspects Angela turning into a witch! Vince's sharp teeth bite his neck, and Tom chokes, lying on the floor. Tom stands up, descending the stairs as the staircase breaks. In such pain, he can't run as his legs become weak from experiencing terrible goosebumps. The family has turned into monsters, which scares the living hell out of him.

The house is moving in different directions. The floor splits, Tom's feet are swelling. Chased by the ghosts of an unearthly moonlight in spasmodic outcry, Tom hears a phantom outside. Tom's heart pounds fast! No idea how to escape evil spirits with his weakness. A nightmare cursed the family. Tom feels he is not a father anymore.

Dashing from place to place with nowhere to hide, hunted by the wraith of ugliness, Tom runs away, escaping the haunted setting to avoid death. Tom knows he's coming to his death through torture.

Tom hides himself in the closet behind the jackets, unseen; rats come from underneath the floor and creep over him! He runs across the living room, breaks through the window, and falls on the flowers. The night sky becomes spookier as a lightning bolt strikes too close, and the house turns into a haunted place within the dark shadows of horror.

For a moment, Tom asks himself, what happened to Joe? In the bushes, he's afraid to sneak out to run fast towards the truck. The grass changes colour from mellow to orange-black; every fallen tree lies dead on the ground. The garden is no longer a living organism. Everything he touches is weird and disgusting—tulips covered in blood, and the backyard turns into a graveyard where the remains of strangers' bodies lay.

Rushing inside the house to find the car keys, he opens the squeaking backdoor—forgetting to close it; inside, Tom hears nothing and spiders crawl over the furniture, ruining it to pieces, making webs. He steps on the creaky wooden floor, pisses in his pants, hears the eerie sounds. Bumps into Joe, seeing his body decapitated! Runs fast, leaving this place behind forever! He makes it through the front doors alive but is trapped behind the gates, which won't open! Cannot figure out an exit strategy.

Thinking quickly, Tom will ram the front gates. An interesting plan! Runs towards the truck parked in the driveway, jumps inside, turns on the engine, and drives through the massive gates, escaping from danger.

Four hundred metres farther, the truck runs out of fuel. Tom sees no parked cars around the neighbourhood! Heartbroken in distress and desperate, Tom wonders if this is how the story ends.

Tom leaves the truck behind with no hope of a safe return home, and the weather persists. Tom walks in the thunderstorm alone with no shelter without seeing a streetlight. His surroundings alienate him in the brutal, dark world.

Unaware of the neighbourhood on Smithson Lane, Tom heads back home, walking fast in darkness, looking for a light at different angles. Nothing! No place to hide from enemies. As a good man with honest faith and naivety, treachery compromised his mind when he bought a house from the lottery winnings and hoped to make himself superior.

He wanders on the puddled street feeling hopeless and shaken by terrible memories; he cannot forget the surrender of his family. The skies lighten with the early morning mist of sunrise; the rain tapers. Tom is soaking wet in his pyjamas, sick with loneliness and no car. He awkwardly makes circles around the property. The house is gone, and the dead rotten land is infested with large crawling bugs, rats, poisonous snakes, and two dead human bodies. His legs hurt from the pain and suffering; in a blink of an eye, Tom sees Angela's remains and Vince's blood on fracked soil! Screams, "What have I done?"

Blood on Tom's dirty hands gives him the creeps, as he touches the bones of an obedient child who turned into a beast; he could not watch the death of Vince—innocent and disciplined. This never would have happened if Tom had exercised proper judgement for his family. It is too late for apologies and his forgiveness of God is obstructed! He leaves his family behind in their graves. This is the price Tom must pay as he lies on the ground, crying in pain.

Chapter 10

The Dragon's Castle of Nottingham

Once upon a time in Nottingham, farmers harnessed the land and brave knights dared to fight fire-breathing dragons. I am Annabella, the daughter of Richard. My father taught me English literature and engaged me to read many interesting novels based on art and folklore. I loved raising farm animals, making new friends, and searching for love. Every night, I read bedtime stories to myself, wrote diaries, and composed impressive songs.

Brought up as a disciplined girl, I was better than the immature children I knew. I wanted to find my partner. My father always wished me the best and supported my future dreams.

I spoke to him, "I want to be married and have children."

This big question silenced him. I knew revealing my secret to Daddy, who raised me as a single parent, would shock him. It surprised me. As my skills grew and I became a young adult, I loved reading fantasy novels, and especially finding a place to write a great story. One evening, I remember singing a wonderful love song aloud to myself.

I came home. "Father, I want to be a princess of Nottingham, to fall in love and to marry someone and live in my castle someday." After this talk, he did not speak to me.

In my heart, I wished it would come to me one day. From that night on, my dream was to become a free girl open to life, exploring the outside world—it's fantasies, finding my true north. One night, the moonlight shone through my window and an angel showed itself.

The angel spoke in a loud voice, "Annabella, you are a fine girl and someone is waiting for a kiss from you. It is your time to continue with your life. I will be with you."

Upset, I said, "How am I going to explain this to my father?"

"Do not worry, I will change your father's mind, freeing you to search for your wish and this will be your quest." The angel vanished.

I had nothing else to say. For the first time, love had taught me a moral lesson. Always find your dream, which will give you the straight path towards success. I would follow my destiny. The next morning, I sat at the breakfast table with my dad, eating fried eggs with toast.

I said, "Dad, I want to find my love in marriage, and someday have children of my own.

Last night, an angel spoke to me, giving me a quest as my last chance to prove myself the bravest, making a new life."

He screamed at me, "You are not going anywhere! You are my daughter and you will stay here with me! Do we understand each other?"

I ran through the fields, crying in pain. In the blink of an eye, I noticed a small tree. I approached it and sat right beside it, crouched in distress. Speechless.

From nowhere, the angel looked and whispered to me, "What is the matter, my darling? Don't listen to your father. I am with you. Follow your dreams." The angel vanished.

The idea that I should not return home came to my mind. A bright sunny day was in forecast and the birds were singing. Alone, with nobody except of my father back home, I decided not to return and to wander off to where my dream would take me. One way to find out. I strolled on the grassland journeying through the fields where I see a dry landscape in front of me.

I continued my pace, heading towards the hillside where daisies bloomed, and I outstretched my arms, relaxed after having a quiet nap under the gorgeous sun. I lay on dandelion fluff and it floated above me as small parachutes which made me sneeze. The breeze blew at my face and I fell sound asleep. I experienced a dreadful dream about marrying a monster and my dad shouting, "Shame on you!!"

I woke up in shock. The fast-moving clouds turned the sky dark. A storm was coming! Thunder rumbled, and I went fast, seeing a spooky forest ahead and the trees shake, trapping me within this terrifying setting with the sounds of hungry wolves! Going deeper into the forest, lost, nowhere to go.

Something creepy touched my shoulder and I was prickly. Screaming from fear, running, I tripped over a sharp rock, looking at the gates in front of me. Lightning bolts fired the dark skies above. I saw a castle and the front gates opened in the blustering winds!

Scared to come inside but knowing danger was close, I had no choice but to make a quiet entry. I opened the squeaking entrance door, closed it. My heartbeat pounded. Inside, a palace in darkness. I saw the shadows of myself walking on the broken tiles surrounded by shattered mirrors and heavy lightning flashes. Wandering around this creepy setting, tired and hungry, I had no clue where I was going. I ascended the stairwell, and the chandeliers shook, and the small windows slammed wide open, making me shiver. To my left, I saw a broken statue, ripped paintings, huge beastly markings on the wall, and blood on the floor behind the curtains. I suspected a dead soldier in his silver armour.

Through the mirror, I saw the dragon's big wings and breath of fire straight at me! Rushing to save my life; the dragon chased me. Too late! I was taken in the dragon's mouth; he carried me, flying to the tallest tower. Lava below me, I was terrified of being drop dead; the dragon pushed me inside a terrifying chamber and locked the doors.

Inside the chamber was a huge gold-plated mirror, a queen-size bed, and a full closet of dresses and elegant skirts for me to wear. Something invisible brought a skirt to me and I undressed myself. There was a cute little dwarf—smart, handsome, and friendly. His name was Tiny Donald.

I heard someone's voice say, "Come and eat."

Tiny Donald explained, "The dragon is the prince cursed by the witch's supernatural power, and he can turn back to a real human if he falls in love with you."

"Will a magic potion help break this spell?"

He responded to me, "No, you are the one who can change this!"

Tiny Donald escorted me from the room to the dragon's dining hall, where I would eat dinner that evening. Descending the uneven stairwell and seeing no handrails in the dark bothered me as a girl not accustomed to living within a haunted castle.

Walking with Tiny Donald to eat dinner, I looked around at the bright chandeliers and I saw a huge royal table and the exquisite antiques. I was trapped as the dragon's guest. I sat at the far end of the table accompanied by Tiny Donald, who would be my server this evening, to serve my meal.

Wrong timing. The floor shook and I heard the roaring of the fire-breathing dragon which scared me! The beast came out and sat, same as a hungry dog! Afraid the dragon might eat me at any moment, I couldn't stand it anymore, and I ran back to my chamber frightened, leaving Tiny Donald.

Myself, a girl who fears monsters, I had nightmares. Lying on the bed, crying in my room, I was scared after the terrible evening. I couldn't imagine not leaving this place alive. It was a matter of time. My life depended on me protecting myself from danger.

Awakened, lighting a candle beside my bed, I stood up, walking towards the window, seeing many shining stars across the night sky, a half-moon, and snow on trees. Feeling the chills, I knew a warm cup of tea would help. How to serve myself? I was afraid to leave my room. It was a question of survival or death. No books to read. I couldn't entertain myself while living imprisoned in a dragon's kingdom situated over hot-boiling lava. Impossible to escape!

Resting on the bed, feeling hungry after many hours of starving, I risked coming back to the dining hall. Leaving my room, closing the squeaking door, I descended the staircase, tip-toeing as my heart-beat pounded fast. Watching my back at every corner, observing my whereabouts to avoid making any dangerous shortcuts. I passed through a broken wall towards a small bridge where I saw water geysers coming out from the burning rocks. Running in the hallway, ambling along the passageway, I looked for a narrow path to take me to the kitchen.

I ran into Tiny Donald.

"What are you doing?"

"I am starving hungry," I whispered.

"Follow me this way, please."

We shared hands tightly to avoid being lost and I made sure I didn't lose my pace. Walking along the steep path towards the dragon's den, we made a left turn, making it to the kitchen. Inside, I saw pots and pans, including golden-plated forks and knives, and lovely plates with exquisite colour which showed an actual reflection of my face. The kitchen looked marble and the shiny floor tiles made this setting an ultimate luxury.

Tiny Donald talked to me in a friendly manner. "Should I prepare you something to eat?"

I said, "I want something delicious to impress me."

Tiny Donald whispered, "I will make you one of the tastiest dishes you've ever tried. It will be a surprise!" I smelled the spicy aromas.

While cooking, Tiny Donald questioned me, "Who are you?"

"I am a single child with a father from a small village in England called Nottingham. I am looking for someone to love me forever. No other place to go except home."

Tiny Donald said, "I told you the prince was turned into a fire-breathing dragon, and if not saved, he will die."

Tiny Donald surprised me. Dinner was ready! I closed my eyes and tasted the dish: mushroom soup in a bread bowl. I couldn't imagine myself falling in love with this beast. I could be dead soon. Out of nowhere, the dragon stomped in, burning the kitchen table!

The beast thundered! He grabbed Tiny Donald by the arm and threw him on the floor! I swung a cast iron pan, hitting the dragon's face. It attacked me, taking me to the lower dungeon! Locked inside the dungeon to never return to my room. This time I cried in pain, shivering from the unpleasantness of sitting on brick in my dress, facing the bars, scared of dying. My life was in great danger if the dragon came to eat me!

I could not sleep inside the dungeon hearing the sounds of hungry crows and the intimidating, howling wolves. Would someone come to my rescue?

Early morning, I saw the rising sun through the tiny window. I had no blanket to cover myself, but the sun's warmth helped me keep my head warm. I sat for hours on the bleak floor, my sore feet making it difficult for me to stand up. The troubles I faced were unpredictable.

I knew I should keep watch for the dragon. I sat on the ground, remembering my father taking me for a quick visit to see the magnificent hillsides where nature helped keep our land sustainable. Everything had changed. I was within this fantasy world, captured, instead of finding my lover! I wondered if I had reached the end.

Good, I had no shackles around my wrists, and no bodyguard. Lucky me! But it was difficult for me to figure out the options of disguising myself to avoid being seen.

In terrible pain, I had no food or water, and the dragon had banned Tiny Donald from coming over to help me. My best friend and warm-hearted person was playing puppet with this monstrous dragon. My captivity was too dangerous and horrifying.

Coughing and sneezing, I lost consciousness. Then, something hot beside my feet. I was awakened lying on the bed with a thermometer in my mouth and a wet towel on my forehead. Resting inside a huge, luxurious royal bedroom, Tiny Donald was taking care of me, and I didn't see the dragon. I couldn't say a word with my strong headache! Not hungry, I experienced dizziness with a high fever, making it difficult for me to concentrate, unable to observe my surroundings where objects spun.

In my bed, suffering from the severe symptoms of weakness and constant changes in body temperature. I closed my eyes and I fell asleep. I could not tell how many hours I slept, having no dreams. Waking up the next morning, I saw Tiny Donald giving me warm tea with candies on the side. He looked sad and silent. I was sorry to see Tiny Donald in his ghastly state. It would be hard for him to take care of me. I stared at the window with blurred vision and, out of nowhere, saw the dragon with roses in its mouth, and he dropped the bunch on the floor.

My eyes close, imagining myself inside the dragon's chamber in my wedding dress, carrying roses, and fire blowing straight at me as I die!

Waking up in shock, having a panic attack, I screamed, "Tiny Donald!"

"It's okay, Annabella, everything is going to be fine."

Tiny Donald held me tight, putting me on the bed as I tucked myself under a warm blanket and covered myself with a nightgown.

I shivered. What a nightmare! Not in the mood to hear a bedtime story, I wanted to be left alone. I was sad to believe I had a sensitive heart—a change from the day I entered through the front gates alone, coming into close contact with the fierce dragon. I couldn't imagine myself going through this horrible stage with no skill and weak perseverance.

Disheartened by terrifying moments, I compromised my future. I would heal myself until I was cured of my illness. The question was, was I ready? In bed, I struggled to figure out ideas, to make tough decisions about risking my life for an escape. Should I stay or run away back home, or give myself a last chance to change everything? I wanted to build a relationship with the dragon.

Tiny Donald convinced me. "The one who can save him is you."

It was too much for me to always lie on my bed. If something went wrong, I was at risk of being killed. The most important question was, what could I do to help myself? I needed a goodnight's rest to have peace of mind before deciding. Sick for days; slow improvement. Alone in my room, under too much stress, feeling ill. My father was not with me anymore. I would protect myself by making the right choices to safeguard my life.

I woke up hearing the music from the hallway, and Tiny Donald playing a musical instrument. A favourable moment came to me when he invited the orchestra inside my room, and a few other well-talented dwarfs sang loudly in front of me! This impressed me. Hitting the last notes, they ended the song with a romantic and cute ending:

"Annabella, the prettiest girl coming to this castle to save the prince's life and us, too."

I looked at them in stunned silence till these dwarfs introduced themselves: Jimmy, Thomas, and Smile. They would now accompany me to forget my sadness. They left the room as I lay on the bed to rest my mind, tired. I asked myself, did these dwarfs fool me into marrying a monster?

I had forgotten my father. Surviving in a horrendous life of tough challenges, I was forgetting who I was, the person who was supposed to stay close to my parent and never abandon my faith. Trapped within the strange world of fantasy and evil, I realized being the dragon's guest had given me unusual fantasies of being a princess.

So, I risked my life to take crazy adventures around the castle, afraid of showing the dragon my charm. Kept within a big castle differed from being back home, where I couldn't go free as an eighteen-year-old girl without my father's permission. I wanted to live alone, away from my dad.

My ambitions told me to follow my dreams and never lose. I thought of changing the dragon's nature from a beast into an actual human; if this happened, I couldn't imagine when I would be friends with the dragon and break the curse, making myself the hero and saving someone who I love most. It was a young girl's dream. My intuition helped me realize the dangers of being seduced by the dragon's evil mind. It was not my nature to be cruel.

My father had taught me to act kind and make friends with good people, no matter the circumstances. Exploring the outside world had made it more dangerous for me. The key challenge was to break the spell.

It would be difficult to escape. I was scared to leave the room and starving hungry. This was crazy! Standing, impatient, I waited for Tiny Donald to bring me food. I was frustrated! This was the time to act serious by not allowing this dragon to kill me. I needed to stay strong by avoiding big troubles.

I was not ready to protect myself from this angry beast. It upset me as a self-reliant person. This journey had taught me to make my own choices while surviving as a girl, assisted by the sweet Tiny Donald, who I admired as a good person. Locked inside my room, I was concerned I was not fit to run on my own, to risk everything with no protection. My father had never taught me the life skills to live alone and did not bring me up to be a "fighting" girl.

It was up to me to decide whether to face the difficulties alone or have Tiny Donald help me change the dragon's behaviour. Would it be possible? I guessed my despicable approach to life was not brave enough to fight against monsters. I was shaping up to be a weak survivor.

But I dared not leave my room without Tiny Donald. I was being kept as a princess, not going anywhere till someone came and rescued me from the fire-breathing dragon. A true story of a girl who couldn't free herself. I understood proving myself by escaping on my own in disguise was crazy, having no power to fight against evil. I was not ready to run alone through the creepy forest. What would my father think when he saw me dressed in my ripped skirt and looking terrible?

The grumbles inside my stomach made me walk around my room, watching through the window at the strange weather. Low cloud cover spun in tornado motion, blowing leaves in spirals. Heavy rain droplets pitter-pattered on the window as thunder rumbled loudly. The howling winds slammed the outside doors. A ghost was roaming somewhere within the castle! Unaccompanied, anxious of being taken by someone's dark shadow, I closed the curtains fast. I stayed inside, afraid to leave my room, locking myself in by putting a chair under the door handle.

Sitting on the chair beside my bed, I remembered my father taking me for a stroll across the farmland where farmers gathered the harvest. Since I was a girl with a soft nature, I had always dreamed of becoming a farmer.

Discomforted by this miserable setting of monsters and strange climate, I was being treated as a prisoner, kept in this castle forever. Fear made my face blush. In the mirror, I saw my hair turning grey! Through my blanket, the bright flashing light made the room turn darker, and a rat crawled over me! I screamed in a night fright, waking after a terrible nightmare! After I had trouble sleeping; silent, I made no sudden movements. Tiny Donald tiptoed towards my bed and pulled the blanket up and saw me scared. I needed comfort with a warm cup of tea.

Tiny Donald whispered, "Annabella, where are you? Are you all right? Do you want another room?"

I had a sudden weakness in my legs while being taken to another room with Tiny Donald's help. Which room would I have?

Tiny Donald carries me. Ascending, I was dizzy from seeing the stairs behind me, hearing strange echoes, which made me have sudden vertigo alongside my psychological trauma.

But I made it, and the room looked smaller but cozy. Inside, everything was empty except for a small bed, a colourful carpet, and a cute little teddy bear sitting on my bed. Tiny Donald and the others put me on the soft mattress, making me comfortable and giving me a wool blanket to help keep me warm. Again, coughing hard, I could not wait till the moment Tiny Donald would bring me hot tea with cookies. I fell fast asleep.

In my imagination, I saw my home becoming a large village where farmers from the countryside brought wholesome foods to my dad standing at the door. Out of nowhere, the fire-breathing dragon came and destroyed everything in its path! Most shocking, the death of my father! Waking up, I saw abundant light within my room and someone knocking at my door. It was Tiny Donald again, who served me a full teapot of delightful aromatic tea, which gave me the craving to have a cookie. My both hands shook after the dream. Speechless.

Tiny Donald consoled me, "Are you feeling better?"

In my tears, I spoke, attuned, "The dragon will soon come in an invasion to kill my father."

Tiny Donald surprised me: "This dragon is good and will kill no one. It is in your imagination. He is waiting till a girl falls in love with him. This will break the curse."

I was astonished, had trouble concentrating on how to answer. I was left alone in my room, not sleeping, and couldn't move beyond my negative thoughts of being the dragon's queen! Why had I chosen this journey as my destiny? This made little sense. It bothered me, thinking about the well-being of my dad. It was too late for an escape!

I recited a silent prayer, asking God to protect my dad and guide me until I was through this misery. One day, I would return home. It would disappoint my father. I lay on the bed staring at the ceiling, silent, and nothing came through an empty mind. Loneliness disheartened me as my cup of tea became lukewarm. The room made me depressed—no hope in this strange world.

I had trusted no one before in my entire life except for my dad, who always took good care of me, and once taught me: "Always believe in yourself and not others. It is your destiny which you choose to fulfill." I still remembered this. Life kept on teaching me the same lessons which I hadn't learned from, not leaving the past behind me. Disappointed, I was not ready. Why had I come?

No sign of anyone. I was left with an empty teapot and the last biscuit on my plate. I had no appetite. The pressures of being imprisoned in a chamber with no open windows, poor lighting, and an empty clothing shelf. I was sick. Darkness had shut in my soul. I was living as a desperate person facing alienation. Would I survive the plight of this misery?

For days, I had trouble sleeping. I stayed awake most of the time looking at a creepy picture of a dying knight burning in flames, hoping I would not be the one standing in fire!

I thought of a brave idea—to meet the dragon. This would be my last chance to prove to my father I was responsible for others and my true heart had compassion and joy. My father would be proud of me if I married a handsome gentleman who was not a monster and could protect me from dangerous enemies. It would be a miracle if the dragon turned back into human form. A life-changing experience to witness.

Someone knocked at my door. I stayed put, sitting on the bed with a teddy bear tucked to my stomach, feeling an unsteady heartbeat. I burst in fear! The squeaking door opened and I saw an enormous shadow! It was Tiny Donald.

He begged me, "The dragon needs your help, my dear! He is in terrible pain and needs you."

I responded, "I am afraid the dragon will hurt me and lock me away forever!"

Tiny Donald said, "I know the dragon much more than you do. You must fall in love to break the spell, bringing a miracle!"

I agreed, "Fine. This time I will try, but if something happens, I am gone!"

I left my chamber in a nice-looking skirt, taking my cute little teddy bear with me as emotional support, and followed Tiny Donald towards the dragon's den. I was moving through wind and fire. Spiders crawled over me within the creepy narrow corridor. I was scared of this haunted setting where I was surrounded by low-flying bats and the sound of wolves. Frightened, my mind told me to not turn back. To prove myself as the bravest girl, I had to stay strong and hold my ground as much as possible, not provoking the dragon and helping myself avoid danger.

As I walked with Tiny Donald along the uneven stairs, I stared at the hot-boiling lava below, which blurred my eyesight. The rope bridge shook and I shared hands with him, holding tight, nervous of falling. It took us a while to cross the bridge.

We approached the main entrance of the dragon's kingdom. As we strolled inside, we stepped over sharp-pointy rocks and rough surfaces. Tiny Donald guided me going through a broken wall of fallen bricks, passing a crumbled stairwell. We were coming closer to the dragon's den! Oh my God! I stood beside Tiny Donald at a huge entrance door, shaking in fear. I opened the door, Tiny Donald and I both looked at the sleeping dragon—a giant, purple-red colour. In the blink of an eye, the dragon woke up, roaring, and breathed fire!

Tiny Donald whispered, "Annabella, calm yourself. Everything is going to be fine. Trust me. I am beside you. Do not worry, please pay close attention."

Tiny Donald shouted, "Shh . . . Danny!"

He introduced me to the dragon. "Danny, remember Annabella? She can work new miracles!"

I knew it! It was a male dragon and a ferocious one! I looked at the dragon's red eye turning wide, and knew he was in pain, the sorrow deep inside him. I sat beside him to give comfort and stayed as close company. Nothing happened! I had met my new best friend!

I knew this beast had no close friends except Tiny Donald, who was kind and generous. The dragon's head lay on my lap, and I stroked it with my sore fingers. It was obvious the dragon needed a close friend with a good nature who appreciated changing him from a beast into a real person.

I've never cuddled a dragon. I saw its sad eyes—this animal needed to be shown dignity and kindness, the connection between women and nature. An interesting perspective. If we make love, I wondered, will the dragon become a real person? I would give the dragon my attention as though he was a first pet! I named him Dragon Danny. I would stay put and not leave this chamber. A wise decision.

I fell asleep beside Dragon Danny, making myself comfortable. I was being cuddled by Danny's long tail, loosened around me. How cute was this? I have a goodnight's rest after the miserable experience back in my room; this time, I have close company and someone to have intimate comfort with. Waking up the next day in the dragon's den alone, I see no sign of Tiny Donald. I didn't see Dragon Danny anywhere; out of nowhere, the ground shook, awakening me as Danny came in flying, bringing a food basket in his teeth. Dragon Danny licked my face—it looked like he was in love with me! This breakfast turned into a romantic morning! A moment I will never forget.

These foods tasted delightful, but were they taken from a market or farm? I hated to ask this question. I would force myself to speak with Dragon Danny—if he would talk. It worried me the villagers might come and kill Danny. We were defenceless! What would happen if they found us? It scared me. Finishing up, Dragon Danny put me on his wing, leaving Tiny Donald behind, and I was flying, seeing the castle below me. The bright sunny sky made for a great early morning flight; breezy winds blew through my hair.

Landing on a hill, I saw a magnificent view of the landscape. Dragon Danny was in a playful mood. The best day of my life. We both played hide-and-go-seek, joyful, and then Danny pushed me on the grass and I stared at clouds in different shapes and forms. Danny sat right beside me, happy, and we spent romantic time together the whole afternoon, making love, kissing and hugging each other. In the late afternoon, we were both hungry for lunch, and Dragon Danny took me back to the castle.

We returned home after a long day; inside, I smelled the fresh foods Tiny Donald had prepared for us. A perfect romantic dinner with lots to eat this evening! At the table, we looked at each other with smiling faces while eating our delicious meal, and Tiny Donald joined us for the special occasion. He was a proper companion and a warm-hearted person to keep us company tonight.

I asked Danny, "Do you want to dance?"

Danny has spoken to me for the first-time and said, "Yes, I would be delighted."

From the dinner table, we went to the ballroom for our first dance together. Approaching, Danny opened the enormous doors. I saw many artistic and colourful paintings.

Danny shouted at me, waving his arms wide, "Everything is yours! You are welcome to my castle and you will become my future queen!"

This castle would one day be mine. I was the lucky one enthroned as Danny's princess, and I couldn't wait for this moment to happen. Inside the ballroom, we started dancing ballet and I remembered how my dad trained me how to dance as an aristocrat. Dancing with Danny felt better than doing household chores for long hours.

After Danny and I danced together, it was midnight and we sat on the wooden bench, keeping each other company, listening to crickets. Tired, we came back inside, locking the backdoors. We walked through the ballroom, going to the kitchen for dessert. I found someone to be with forever! With no life experience, I was proud of my accomplishment.

Dragon Danny brought me a tall cake prepared by Tiny Donald and a nice bottle of wine to celebrate our first date this evening! I have a small bite of this delicious cake topped with lots of whipping cream, chocolate, and strawberries, which tasted as sweet as frosted caramel, better than wine. Back home, I had never eaten this well.

Remembering the hardships of home saddened me. I was not in the mood for love, a young girl who was heartbroken and had never been free to live her own life. But I did well for myself becoming someone who deserved to be given the best opportunity: my companionship with Tiny Donald and a warm relationship with Dragon Danny. I hoped this would last longer.

I had much to say to Dragon Danny about our future, about being king and queen for the rest of our lives. Tired after a long day, I accompanied Dragon Danny to the master's bedroom to make love. I couldn't wait till the moment of my dreams—when Danny turned into an actual human by breaking the curse and proposing to him before the wedding day!

I ascended the stairs. Approaching the massive doors and opening them, I saw a chandelier made of genuine diamonds, above a huge king-sized bed! A big room. Undressing myself before going to bed, I lay and tried to get comfortable as my stiff back worsened along with the soreness in my leg muscles. But it was the time to enjoy myself. We made love with the lights off, and I fell asleep. While dreaming, I saw my dad bringing an entire war party to look for me. Archers stormed inside the castle, shooting at us! I woke up screaming into a walking nightmare!

I heard a loud voice from downstairs: "Where is my daughter?!"

Dragon Danny was not in my room, and I couldn't find him anywhere. Dressing myself quickly to search for Tiny Donald, I ran downstairs, "Danny!!" I was grabbed strongly by the left arm and was my father!

He screamed at me, "Where have you been? I searched you for months and you never came back, leaving me behind in struggle and loneliness! How could you do this to me?!"

I cried, "I hate you!"

In tears, looking for Dragon Danny, I rushed in fear and heard an enormous roar! Dashing fast! I approached the door and saw a group of men arrowing at Dragon Danny. "No!!" He lay on the ground suffering as dark blood splattered the floor! I pet him in comfort with tears in my eyes.

On the spot, I kissed Danny's lips. "Please don't leave me! I love you."

These men stood behind me. Dragon Danny turned fast into an actual human and the curse was over. I had saved the life of a warm-hearted person! Surrounded by others looking at me, shocked. It looked like I broke the witch's incantation!

I saw Danny, a vigorous man who dwelled in spirits, reborn as a nice-looking person who I dreamed of marrying. Danny was my future king. My father stormed in, pushing the villagers aside, and punched Danny.

I tried to stop the fight, screaming, "Please, Father, don't break my heart!"

He screamed at me, "You are my daughter and we are leaving, away from this place!"

I grabbed Danny's hands, standing up for him. "No, I am not leaving! He is mine! I am in love with Danny and I am not leaving him!"

The emotional villager supported me. "Come on, Richard! Your daughter is a sweetheart.

She needs someone grateful to love her and be with forever till the end of time! Danny deserves her! If you will go against her wishes, we are no longer brothers."

My dad looked at us with contempt. "I wonder if you want this."

Blushing, I responded, "Yes." Tears filled my eyes with excitement. The others cheered, "Let us have a fiesta!"

I left the chamber for the ballroom, and my dad and the villagers joined. I heard classical music, everyone having champagne and desserts in celebration. My dad sat on a chair drinking alone.

I went to him. "What is the matter? Give me a chance to explain. I love Danny with my heart and please let me marry him and you will have grandchildren and we will live happy. Please, Dad!"

Daddy accepted. "Yes, my sweetheart. I will allow you to live on your own."

I responded, "Thanks dad. Enjoy the party and have fun. Come, join us!"

We returned to the ballroom to celebrate this special night as family and friends. Danny was waiting for me beside a table. He took my hand as we approached the center, beginning our first dance together. Everyone looked at us, ready for the ball. I heard loud applauses which made me happy as a talented dancer.

I danced fast, seeing everything spinning around me, dizzy from this wild partying. The fun continued. One of my heels fell off and I lost my balance, falling over and Danny held me as we kissed each other and my father's face changed. Love at first sight! Danny helped me to stand on both feet. By morning, I was tired of celebrating. The castle's clerestory was glowing with light from the sunrise.

I urged, "Danny, please take me to the room."

He carried me in his arms and I fell asleep! A few hours later, I woke up inside my bedroom. I heard my father speaking to Danny. I came and sat on the sofa, listening to Daddy's words.

"Annabella, you are too young to marry. Your marriage with him is out of the question."

I argued, "No, Dad! Danny is mine, and we will be together for the rest of our lives."

How could my father break his promise? I didn't know he was so stubborn; I thought he could change to become a better person. My mistake. Sitting in the kitchen with Danny, we both discussed our future together, which made us think about our children—if the spell could pass onto them. Our relationship worried me. I wanted to live a happy life with wealth and children, not be troubled by a parent's ego.

I was angry—I had no chance to love someone, and Daddy behind my back, giving me orders! Danny and I faced many challenges. It was going to be tough to convince my father again. Suddenly, I hear an awful racket and we both rushed, seeing a witch flying on a broomstick, casting a spell on Daddy!

Danny shouted, "Stop! Leave him alone! It is you again, Witch Agnes!"

She yelled from above, "Dragons don't live happily ever after!!" Then she cast her wand, unleashing a deadly spell upon Danny. Daddy interfered to save Danny's life and lay on the floor unconscious! I cried on the spot.

Danny screamed at Witch Agnes, "You will pay for this!" He grabbed his sword to fight.

The witch laughed, looking at Danny. "You will never catch me!"

I watched him risking his life to take revenge, proving his bravery was strong enough to protect me from evildoers. Above me, the witch flew on her broomstick, throwing explosives at us and the castle turned into a wild jungle of bloody-thirsty wolves scaring the living hell of me. In a blink of an eye, in the most epic moment I ever saw, Danny charged the witch and jumped high, clutching his sword, and killing Witch Agnes! Danny fell on the floor, hurt.

I kissed him. "You are my hero and thank you for saving my life! I will marry you!"

Daddy, as a horse, approached us, speaking in his authentic voice. "Danny, Annabella, you both deserve each other! I bless both of you."

For days we planned our wedding: cleaning the castle, mopping and wiping the windows and polishing the wooden furniture. We found a priest to lead the ceremony, and we had a few people to help us redecorate, sew clothes, finding a chef to prepare table foods, and much more! The others helped us with organizing the main entrance for the guests. I found a marvellous picture in a glass frame.

"I drew this painting for you and is yours to keep," said Danny. I kissed him. "Thank you, my love. I will hang it in my room."

On the day before the wedding, we started early in the morning preparing the ballroom, deciding which foods to put on the big table; cake and champagne for everyone! It disappointed me, being an eighteen-year-old with no brother or sister. Except for a few guests and my father, I had no friends and no family.

We completed our duties and were prepared for tomorrow's wedding day. Ready for a goodnight's rest, Danny and I headed to bed exhausted. Half-asleep while Danny snored, I couldn't stop thinking about tomorrow's wedding and how there would only be with few guests.

I woke up the next morning after little sleep, appearing less energized than yesterday. Danny was not in the room. Where was he? Suddenly, a group of bridesmaids came from nowhere, introducing themselves: Martha, Gloria, Carolyn, Susanna, and Ms. Goldberg. Real hairstylists and fashion designers, the best. I didn't know who hired them. It couldn't be Danny. It looked like my father had planned this for me! A big surprise.

I was ready! I watched myself in the tall glass mirror, dressed in a gorgeous wedding dress, and Ms. Goldberg gave me a nice pair of heels. Accompanied by the bridesmaids helping me downstairs, I walked on high heels for the first time. I had waited a long time for something good to happen—my wish had come true!

Walking on the carpet, approaching the ballroom, I didn't see Danny. A few minutes later, he showed up, dressed in a well-tailored, black suit. It was time! The bridesmaids guided us to the chapel. We shared hands while walking, seeing an old priest holding a prayer book in his hands, ready to begin the ceremony. It looked weird seeing my father as a horse. He stared at us but we paid no attention.

I listened to the priest's recitation: "Annabella, will you take Danny to be your husband?"

I smiled, "I do."

The priest repeated, "Danny, will you take Annabella to be your wife?"

Danny replied, "Yes, I do."

Danny gave us the wedding rings, and we kissed each other. We left the chapel, heading back to the ballroom as a married couple! Everyone saw through the window. The forest turned enchanted and werewolves turned into friendly huskies. We celebrated throughout the evening!

A year later, we had our first child, and his name was Samuel. We lived in the castle in prosperity for the rest of our lives. I will always remember: if you follow your own dreams, life will take you towards a straight path. It is your destiny which you choose.

Chapter 11

A Convicted Serial Killer

In 1980, Samantha is a ten-year-old orphan living in Blumburg, a poor class neighbourhood where crime concerns her. Samantha never had parents to protect her from strangers. Blumberg has become more dangerous than ever since Samantha was born. Many killings reported on the news each day. Beside the orphanage, Samantha is afraid of attending school, where she sees police officers run with their handguns.

Samantha was afraid to fight dangerous thugs. She's seen the violence of people being beaten. It made her into a weird person, always locking herself at home.

One day, she hears the broadcast about a serial killer escaped from jail wandering, unseen, the streets of Blumburg. His name was Carl Mann. Others living in the hometown are concerned the lives of children are at risk. Cannot imagine the dangers of being caught by this psychopath who fears no one and kills. Samantha stays in her suite, planning an escape as she waits to be called for breakfast. It's Samantha's last day at the orphanage, as she's preparing herself for this night's escape. Criminals bother her when speaking with others in public, makes her have no appetite. Samantha overhears someone knocking at the door and she hides herself under the bed, and a janitor comes inside, mopping the floor, and her heart pounds fast, and he walks out. Lucky!

Samantha spends hours thinking of strategies to avoid being caught by the guards downstairs. This crazy idea worries her as a kid with no life experience, troubled by a dangerous person. Samantha has a risky chance to jump three floors below without being spotted.

Samantha takes her teddy bear with her, leaving the clothes behind, and leaves wearing an old sweater in ripped Levi jeans. Dark and quiet. She opens the window. She stands on the window-sill, holding her balance, and jumps, falling three floors, making a soft landing on an enormous pile of stinky garbage.

She stands on the sidewalk in her disgusting pants, running away from the orphanage to avoid the serial killer. She approaches the intersection. Out of nowhere, Carl Mann, in disguise in front of the church grabs Samantha. He throws her inside a stolen car and drives away fast.

Kidnapped, trying to open the rear door, Samantha sees Carl pointing a gun at her. "Shut up!" Sitting on the backseat, she tucks her teddy bear on her stomach. Ten minutes later, the car stops, and he opens the rear door, drags Samantha, and tapes her mouth. She has trouble breathing from the tape gagged around her head. She sees no streetlights and darkness everywhere; the car speeds and loses control! Carl reloads his pistol. Samantha screams.

He threatens her, "You scream again, I will kill you!"

Samantha can't say a word to shut out his foul language. Fear of dying bothers her; she's a girl in big trouble, trapped in the horrors of abuse. She's constipated by psychological pressures, sweating from fear, terrified of what might happen if Carl pulls the trigger.

Samantha is driven far away from home and misses sitting in her room, protecting herself. She realizes being kidnapped has taught her a fine lesson never to leave the orphanage. She guesses it's too late for a return; Carl will keep her abducted till someone pays a ransom.

The car makes a sharp right turn, goes over a pothole, and Samantha bumps her forehead as she crouches on the back seat, thinking to open the back door; terrible news, the door locks! Damn it! No other choice but to wait for the opportune moment to free herself.

Samantha is under a close watch. Carl carries a handgun in his right pocket. Samantha cannot afford to make any sudden movements. Inside the car, feeling uncomfortable, she is an innocent young person kept in torture by this maniac who has no respect for others. Risking life to be brave, she must pay the price to defeat this serial killer. If not, she will face death as guns scare her.

She's defenceless, with no survival experience to fight a madman who committed heinous crimes and has no care for someone else's freedom. Afraid of making any sound, Samantha looks through the window, seeing a deserted land, a perfect place for a silent kill. She's been kidnapped inside the car for hours. Hungry and thirsty, she shakes from the fears of violence.

He brakes the car. Samantha falls from the backseat, bruising herself. Moments later, he hits her on the head with the butt of his handgun. Samantha faints on the spot! Awakening, she's tied to a chair, gagged in thick rope. A strong neck pain causes Samantha to have a terrible headache from the hit. Dizzy, she's experiencing a sudden weakness.

Samantha recovers and finds she's locked inside a stinking locker room filled with roaches, and large flies sting her itchy skin into red blisters. She screams. A squeaking metallic door opens, and Carl approaches her with his two-inch folding knife, cuts the ropes, and grasps Samantha's right arm, dragging her through the creepy hallway. The other prisoners watch at her being mistreated. They laugh. She is ashamed.

Carl kicks Samantha, and she falls to the ground. "Leave me alone!" Samantha moans.

Carl screams, "You are my hostage and you will obey everything I tell you!"

Samantha is being pushed inside a minivan with no underwear and a dirty t-shirt. Abuse turns her into a young female victim used for plunder! She sees the bruises on her right leg and knee, in serious pain as blood drips from the kneecap and arms. Carl ties her to the backseat, wrapping the seatbelt around her back as Samantha squats, facing the trunk. The van drives fast as she watches the prison left behind in dust. She experiences a stomach ache for many miles with no water and no food. Samantha cannot take it anymore!

She recognizes the red minivan; in the rear, Samantha spots handguns, a few loaded machine guns, and cigarette boxes. With no clue what to do, she's trapped in a dangerous setting, confused whether to make an escape or stay put while waiting till the police come and arrest him. The minivan speeds on the highway, and cars honk. Samantha is afraid to piss on the seat. Samantha does not know what will happen if Carl shoots her. Unable to call for help, she is frightened!

It is midday, and the long highway looks empty. She sees no cars, just a ghost road taking them nowhere. He will use Samantha as his false daughter, taking her to different places, or worse.

No way out of this misery. Samantha is in great danger of being taken and no one will find her. Her health is at the most vulnerable risk of death! Can she stop this from happening? How will Samantha survive this alone, if Carl becomes more dangerous?

She sits on the backseat, shivering in fear, and hungry for twenty-four hours in ripped clothing and smelly, wet underwear, she tries not to fall asleep. Is Samantha headed towards a safe path? She prepares for an escape while she avoids provoking him and making no mistakes. It will be difficult for her.

She looks through the window, seeing many spruce trees beyond the hillside, no cars, and wildlife. Passing through a gate, she spots a small lodge, sees smoke coming out from the chimney. Makes a sharp right turn, Carl drives over rocks as the minivan's wheels wobble. He comes out of the car in anger, opens the sliding door, and throws Samantha on the ground; she lands on her stomach and he grabs her, unlocking the door of his lodge.

Inside the lodge, Samantha sees mice everywhere and becomes frightened when suddenly Carl punches her and leaves her lying on the floor, bleeding, and does not help her! Such a disgrace of an animal who shows no respect for anyone! Never in her entire life has she been treated like this.

How long will Samantha survive? If she makes any dangerous moves, she will end up in the grave. What Samantha will do if he takes her to places where criminals traffic young girls and kill them? She thinks fast with precautions, not provoking this maniac. He will never change. Samantha will be always an orphan. One day, will she leave these horrors behind and live in freedom or wait for adoption?

Samantha helps herself up from the sharp nails detached on the wooden floor, finds one stuck in her skin. She smells blood dripping from her arm! Sits on the floor in despair and hears the squeaky tread of Carl's crocodile leather shoes and reacts.

He takes Samantha! "Stand up, you lazy prick! I don't have time!"

He places his revolver at her forehead. She stands up in pain and cannot walk from the swelling ankles. Walks on bare, dirty feet. The serial killer closes the backdoor and threatens Samantha to march.

The snow calms her swollen feet while making small footsteps. Surrounded by evergreens, Carl is behind Samantha's back, and she fears walking along this strange path to nowhere. Samantha has a brilliant idea to run when he's not spying! Walks for over five kilometres as her bare feet become frozen.

Carl talks to Samantha in his sore voice, "Don't move!"

At the right moment, he runs inside the bushes. This is Samantha's chance to escape! She escapes in the blizzard through the woods, spots an abandoned tent, a brilliant spot to spend the night alone. Finds a sheepskin coat beside a half-emptied whisky bottle, having a small drink to warm-up herself. Samantha tucks herself in this furry coat and falls asleep.

Dreams, awakens in another terrible nightmare of Carl finding her hiding in the tent and shooting her. She wakes past midnight and fears moving to another place at this hour, the dangers of running and being hunted by territorial groups. Samantha decides not to risk her life and waits till morning to avoid trouble. Again, being captured is not her death wish.

In the morning, the radiant sunrise shines across the forest where spruce trees grow tall, and the wintry sky make her relax. Samantha's mission is to examine her surroundings, not by running from corner to corner. She needs to hide and continues further, know it is risky for her survival if she's caught at the wrong place.

Samantha roams through the forest, trapped within a maze with no way out, fearing Carl is following her. Samantha's intuition tells her she should not stop and move forward till she's through with this horrendous escape; she must always remember to stay cautious while walking, which will be one of her most arduous task.

Running to look for another hiding spot, she spots a wild river. Downstream, rocks are hard to cross over. She stands on the fertile ground, guessing where to go. Rests on the stepping-stones, with no idea where to head next, confused about whether to go back or risk skipping through the fast-moving water. Samantha heads downstream along the trail, crossing the shallow river.

Thirsty, Samantha crouches beside the river and drinks the cool, sweet water. The best day of her life to live alone, away from criminals. She stands up, walking on the stepping stones, keeping a steady balance to avoid a fall; the slippery ground makes her feet frozen with no shoes. Samantha looks at her footprints, afraid Carl will find her.

She sees a tall mountain and continues her path towards a steep cliff, climbing to the furthest top, which will be her rest stop for today. The wonderful sunset lightens the north skies; it's dark outside, no flashlight and no tent. The glowing stars above. She sees beyond the hillside, a distant horizon, a new world is present.

Samantha wonders whether to walk farther or stay put till morning. Afraid of exploring new sites, she is too blind to understand the challenges of surviving alone, as her days of enjoying herself in freedom are ending. Samantha squats on the wet grass, thinking of other ways to hide. She is being followed. She cannot imagine if someone comes out in the middle of the night and grabs her for a silent kill. She fears of falling asleep.

Not scared of darkness, just dangerous company. She falls asleep in a strange dream, imagines herself running within a fantasy world where bandits chase her, and ends up stuck on a volcanic; below her, lava bursts. Wakes up in shock. An unexpecting surprise: a poke behind her back and she blacks out! Someone carries Samantha's body; she has trouble recognizing this person. Hours later, her eyes half-open, she looks around with blurred vision, again kidnapped— now inside a white BMW with a few dangerous guys pointing a gun at her ribs. Samantha sees Carl is the driver!

Her forehead sweats; she's terrified of death. Riding along the empty road, through dust and sand, pitch black outside, Samantha's compassion for life is dead. Violence has shattered her self-nature as she experiences the threats of guns and knives. The dark side of life gave Samantha no survival experience; now, she'll be kidnapped forever with no idea if she will return home, guessing this will not happen.

Samantha sits on the seat handcuffed, experiences the excruciating pain in her wrists. Treated much worse than a dog. As she attempts to free herself, these criminals threaten to kill her, and she cannot fight them. Scared of falling asleep on the bandits' lap, terrified of making any sudden moves, she has negative thoughts about a walking nightmare. The strange road to nowhere. Carl drives the sports wagon with an ego, is a brute with foul language when he hits the steering wheel many times. Samantha is panic-stricken. Cries in pain, and her tears fall on the leather seat.

Any moment could turn dangerous for Samantha. She must wait until a lucky moment happens. Each second of being kept under threat, afraid of staring at the bandit holding his knife, Samantha experiences hysteria. Confusion blankets her mind with terrible thoughts of whether she'll live or die. She hates to picture herself being assaulted on the highway and left behind brutalized to death. Samantha prays, "God, please help me and take me home."

A lucky moment happens! Out of nowhere, the sirens of a police car. Samantha looks through the rear window and Carl opens the front door, shooting; she ducks, covering both ears. The glass window shatters over her! They crash, hitting a large pothole and the car rolls over a few times on the road beside big rocks!

Police officers rush with guns. "Don't move! On your knees!"

The police officers approach the car and drag the men out—they lie flat on the road, detained! The moment Samantha had been waiting! An RCMP officer opens the door and gives his hand.

He introduces himself as Officer Simon Gram. He escorts Samantha to his squad car and an ambulance approaches; paramedics come out running straight towards Samantha, putting her on the gurney, and she falls asleep. It is over, and she will leave this craziness behind, forgetting the kidnap. She is on a different path to start her own life. This will be her foremost challenge to decide.

Comatose, Samantha has flashbacks of being kidnapped and fear sweeps through her. She goes through the serious trouble of the last forty-eight hours of misery and neglect. Never in her whole life has she seen the dark side of a serial killer's terrible greed.

Samantha wakes up in the hospital feeling unwell and sad. No one to keep her company. She hears a patient in the hallway screaming, scaring others in their beds half awake in shock! A social worker comes with the doctor and he opens the curtains and introduces himself as Dr. Manfred.

Dr. Manfred speaks with Samantha in private. "You have a knee fracture, and many bruises. This is Tina, your social worker." He leaves.

Tina questions Samantha, "Do you want to live in a foster home?"

Samantha whines, "Yes, doctor, I want to be dismissed from hospital."

Tina says, "Ok, you will leave tomorrow to meet your foster parents, but you will have to be in a wheelchair."

"Thank you." Samantha coughs.

It's difficult for Samantha to forget her worst life and the insecurity of being a lonely survivor left hopeless. Eating her meal in silence, enjoying every moment of privacy, she turns on the television, watching a comedy show. Samantha encounters many terrible memories of having no family. This one she remembers: Gabriella Johnson, her step-sister, went missing after coming home from a disco party. It happened on the evening of March 15, 1975. She was abducted by a group of young men in their late twenties driving a classic car. No one caught them. Five years later, and the detectives still haven't resolved this case and Gabriella has not been found.

Samantha is admitted from hospital the next day, in the wheelchair, she sees two foster parents waiting beside the front reception! They take Samantha to her new home.

Chapter 12

The Mars Expedition

Imagine yourself as a cosmonaut visiting different planets and lost within a strange world where the risk of death is high. What if there's no chance of returning home?

Jack Dem, a quantitative researcher at the University of California, dreamed one day to fly airplanes and become a pilot. When he was promoted as one of NASA's best researchers, his career improved. Now, Jack waits for the greatest moment of his lifetime. On a late Monday afternoon, Humphry steps in for a private talk, and speaks to Jack:

"You impress us with your investigations and your research. For the past fifteen years, we have appreciated your help with the team. We are offering you an exciting opportunity to travel to Mars and conduct a research project by examining life on Mars. You will report your discoveries to your teammate. We classify this assignment of yours as a top-priority, four-month mission. Expect intense training to prepare you well for this exciting trip. Are you ready to take this journey?"

Jack agrees, "Yes, sir."

Jack is nervous, and his hands shake. He knows it will be his first major career accomplishment. He's proud of what he does, using his willpower to achieving any target goals with self-motivation and approaching new challenges.

On the first day of training, Jack starts his fitness tests and completes the neuropsychological assessment. After a week of harsh exercise at the NASA Johnson Space Center in Houston, Texas, Jack is worried about leaving his family. Floating in gravity inside a shuttle is a challenge for those putting their lives at risk.

Tomorrow at 10 am, Jack will launch to Mars, and he heads home, preparing himself. After a busy workday, he knocks and Carolyn opens the door it with a big smile on her face.

"Come in, supper is ready," she calls out.

Jack walks into the bedroom, looking worried about telling everyone the sad news. He's not hungry, and the anxiety makes him cry. He hides himself in the washroom. The children don't want to see him crying.

Fifteen minutes later, Carolyn says, "Jack, dinner is ready."

She searches everywhere for him until she opens the door and sees Jack weeping.

"What is the matter?"

Whimpering, he says, "I am leaving tomorrow morning for my first expedition to Mars. How will you survive alone for a full year?" She is heartbroken and leaves Jack.

Under pressure, Jack can't sacrifice this trip, especially without losing his reputation. He falls asleep lying on the bathroom floor for an hour; later, he sleepwalks across the bedroom, hitting himself hard on the bedside table. Jack wakes up and stares at his wristwatch. It is past midnight. Packs his suitcase with the important items needed to survive, including research supplies and lots of writing stuff, to record data in a detailed report. These preparations take hours, until early morning. No sleep.

Jack dresses himself in his astronaut uniform, ready for a ride to the Kennedy Space Center in Florida—departing to Mars. Before leaving, he has thirty minutes to eat breakfast; in the kitchen, his family eats in silence. Jack grabs a plate, taking a few pancakes, and the fresh coffee, which fills the air with great aroma. He knows sending postcards or letters will not happen.

Finishing, Jack packs his belongings beside the door before a tough moment of giving hugs and warm kisses. A taxi honks its horn, and someone comes from the space station to pick him up before departure. Two hours remaining.

Inside, Jack asks the driver, "Can my family join with me?"

"Sorry. We are going through a restricted zone," he responds. No argument.

Jack kneels, hugging his sons tight. "Please listen to your mother and take care of each other till I return."

He brings his suitcase, closing the car door, and orders, "Let's go."

At the military base, Jack climbs the ladder and inside the cockpit is the captain, a young lady named Martha Stevenson. A professional in spaceflight technology. Jack and Martha shake hands, preparing themselves, and wait to hear from the control tower. Ten minutes later, they have permission for launch. The rocket's engine blasts as they're pushed back in the upright position facing the windshield. They find themselves in liftoff, breaking through the mesosphere where the environment turns darker. They are travelling in outer space. It is Jack's first time observing the Milky Way— seeing a white blanket of shining stars.

Jack's job is to retrieve data, give exact coordinates, and report their progress. Trained astronauts complete duties to improve research, which he prepared before this trip.

They travel for three months, heading towards the sun. Jack and Martha both know difficult moments are dangerous when a planet orbits; their lives are at risk if they give inaccurate coordinates and false calculations. No shortcuts in time, and making wrong guesses is not an astronaut's method.

Half a year after they left Earth, one of their fears is darkness bringing them into a volatile planet with no life. As cosmonauts, making it to Mars quicker is impossible—the universe itself is spacious. Long travel requires patience and hard work keeping a close eye on alien ships and giant meteorites. They are both on this difficult and dangerous mission together.

They look through the window and see an immense magnetic storm covering the space shuttle, and clusters of aluminium paint float in thin gravity. Jack reacts fast to manoeuvre the space shuttle to save their lives!

Jack panics. "The rocket's engines are burning!"

Martha responds, "We have three months left of travelling to Mars, and we should break the sound barrier."

In the cockpit, they fire up the rocket's engine and the blast of its powerful force leaves behind a massive spread of stardust. Jack and Martha hold hands, moving faster than the speed of light, breaking the record from the earlier explorations. They have been travelling in space for six months and should arrive in a few weeks, depending on their progress. Jack hopes they have enough fuel.

The time comes! They hear a beeping signal and they detect Mars on the radar. Flying through solar winds of stardust makes it difficult for them to land in zero visibility. Making a rough landing on solid ground, stumbling over tiny, sharp rocks, they crush into a small mountain beside an abandoned post.

Jack is awake. Research supplies and food resources are gone. Martha's head is lying on his lap! Jack shakes her twice—unresponsive! He kicks the spacecraft's hatch open, takes the oxygen tanker and carries Martha. Then he puts the umbilical cord to her mouth to save Martha. Jack tries to connect with NASA's telecommunicators, but it's too late. She is dead! Seconds later, behind a rock, the shuttle explodes into flames.

Jack cannot see through heavy smoke and the red sand filths the air with ash and burned fuel, making it difficult to breathe through the umbilical cord. He runs fast in his astronaut suit towards the abandoned post, looking at a Perseverance Rover—a space vehicle designed to collect findings related to life on Mars. Jack made a mistake coming here, risking his life.

With no spacecraft to head back home and no satellite communications to reach NASA Headquarters, Jack is desperate. His luggage items burned into flames. Inside the post, he finds water and no food, only old clothing and a ripped two-fold mattress. Jack thinks he will succeed by storing weapons as a potential way to protect himself from space invaders. The question which remains unknown is whether he'll win a fight against aliens and destroy every cornerstone. The choice is survival or death.

On Mars, Jack organizes his post and keeps everything in order before heading out on his first spacewalk, risking to do fieldwork, analyzing the dangerous climate on Mars. If spotted by UFOs, Jack's life will be in peril; he looks around at his surroundings, exposed to eminent threat.

In his dirty spacesuit, Jack drives the Perseverance Rover on a rocky surface of red dirt and sand dunes created by powerful solar winds in the extreme climate. After a half hour of doing field research, Jack is in a severe sandstorm. His Perseverance Rover is stuck under a big rock. Welcome to hell! Leaves his vehicle behind with no place to hide from dangerous weather events. Saving himself from blowing dust, he hears tons of sand pellets hitting the helmet—much worse than a torrential rainstorm!

A Dead End

Jack wanders off with trouble breathing, feeling a decrease in his oxygen supply. He's on the verge of dying from suffocation. Walks in exhaustion with no Perseverance Rover. Sees a dazzling red flash where UFOs drop from their flying saucer, firing lasers at his post!

Risking life if he attacks them, Jack finds no way out. He is faced with a serious challenge. Jack must keep strong by defending himself from enemies at any attack. His post burns in flames with no defence mechanism. He finds a rocket launcher and aims it at a precise angle, taking a direct shot at the flying saucer, and it explodes into pieces!

Jack's Safe Return Home

No point in staying with nothing. A radio transmission line connects with NASA. Jack presses the call button and waits.

"My name is Jack Dem. Martha is dead! I have no food and I want to return home."

One of NASA's telecommunicators notifies him, "We are sending a backup space shuttle that is coming close to Mars and will arrive in a week."

Jack waits. A week later, the space shuttle finally descends! He runs towards it, climbs the rope, and jumps. The space shuttle takes off, leaving Mars behind! After another 290 days of travel, Jack lands in Florida—at the Kennedy Space Center. A few hours later, after the long car ride, Jack reunites with his family! The next day, Jack steps inside Humphry's office.

Jack talks, "Humphry, Martha Stevenson is dead, and I have no research findings. My evidence is gone. The next time you send me on a mission, please assign me to a bigger group of highly trained astronauts!"

Humphry argues, "Jack, you chose this mission yourself. Don't blame me for your incompetence. I thought you could be a great addition to the team—my mistake. You are not a good astronaut, and in this case, I am firing you! Don't you ever insult your superiors again! Get out of here!"

Jack punches him. "You bastard!"

Jack leaves the office with a scowl on his face. A day spent arguing. He's disappointed in himself; he made the wrong choice to abandon his family for nothing. Humphry must pay for this! The worst moment Jack encountered was having to survive the challenges on Mars without any help.

Jack walks on the busy street, not taking the bus. As an experienced astronaut, he learned something about being a brave survivor after Martha's death—he defeated the aliens for the first time. It turned him into a stronger man to fight fearsome enemies. Jack is proud of what he accomplished.

Jack returns home after this heart-breaking day, in a sad mood with nothing to say. His family is happy to see him; they want to spend good quality time with Daddy. This changes when Jack's wife speaks. "What is the matter, my darling?" He ignores her and goes straight to the bedroom to rest. That evening, he does not join them. Jack acted like a fool, tempered by the dysfunctional Humphrey who showed him no respect. Many regrets come to mind.

Asleep, experiencing the flashbacks of Martha's death, Jack wakes up early morning, having slept well. Not hungry for breakfast, he goes downstairs to the living room where he hears a phone ringing and his wife answers.

She calls, "Jack, someone wants to talk to you!"

He picks the phone up and listens. "Jack, we are offering you a new work position at the Kennedy Space Center. Want to join?"

Jack knows he was fired yesterday, and speaks, "Let me think." He drops the call.

His wife says, "What was it about?" Jack walks out without a word.

Jack sits on the bench in the backyard, decides no. He will leave no one. His career is over—he is no longer an astronaut. He's made a moral decision to forget everything and focus on a new career. Jack returns home, announces to his family that he is quitting his job and will spend most of his time with the happier and stronger family!

Chapter 13

Las Vegas in Sandy Valley

My Early Life

Have you ever wished to dream big, ever wanted a different life? In my early years as an underaged kid banned from casinos, I watched a late evening tv show on how Las Vegas was built on a deserted land, surrounded by sand dunes and exotic desert amphibians. I heard the casinos attracted tourists from heat to chilled indoors, events, boozing at the lobby bar. For underage fools have a dream to dress inconspicuously as adults to sneak inside the casino and enjoy the world of fantasy and win prizes.

I dream I will win a large sum of money, enough to buy a new bike for myself and impress my friends. I see poker tables and slot machines, and well-dressed servers wandering around to serve guests refreshments, especially those rich guys smoking their Cuban cigars. I've never played cards. I am a straight-forward person who is curious to imagine the genuine men's life.

I have aspirations of exploring different places with excitement. I deserve a spontaneous holiday. As an adopted child living under harsh discipline, I miss my friends and stay at home most of the time under a close watch. I want to break away from hardship and non-stop arguments that make me want to leave home and never come back.

A Long Journey

I have this crazy idea to sneak out of my room at midnight wearing this Halloween costume of mine, which I designed. Before heading out, I see myself in front of a mirror—staring at this mediocre costume of mine, I laugh.

I jump out from the window, tiptoeing on the roof to avoid waking the whole neighbourhood. I drop onto the driveway, and my step-father yells, carrying his shotgun, and I run fast towards a taxicab.

I shout, "Stop the cab! Don't go!" Gun shots fire a few hundred metres away.

I open the taxi door. "Take me to Las Vegas!!"

"Yes, boy! My name is Mike." Inside the car, I am relieved with a big smile. I whoop.

Mike says, "Do you have money with you, boy?"

Checking inside my side pockets for spare change, I whine, "I am sorry. I have no cash."

Mike stops his taxicab and lets me go. In tears, I am stranded on the road, with nothing except a small suitcase. I sit on the grass, watching for another automobile to take me. Hours pass and still no sign of any approaching cars. I give up, walking in fear this strange route could be the wrong way to Las Vegas. Risking my life to search for shortcuts is my last resort.

I wander on the road, seeing no exit signs, taking precautions. Rocky mountains surround me. The hot humid air from the north-west side. Less than a half-kilometre away, going in deep potholes, I notice a deserted gas station and a salvage car. I make a quick run, sprinting with excitement, hoping to find something to eat. Near the gas station, I stand in the parking lot, seeing large dinosaur footprints. Strange. A joke—I think I am in the wrong place, somewhere isolated within Arizona. I approach the gas station, opening the front doors, looking inside for foodstuff. I hear an awful roaring sound.

I rush outside, seeing a real tyrannosaur storming toward me, hungry for breakfast. Spotting a station wagon, an old Cadillac Biarritz, I try starting the engine several times—it's not working! I find a propane barrel and lit it with a cigarette lighter and run away to save my life. A few moments later, an outburst of heavy flames and sand blows over me!

Freeing myself from a deep burial, I stand up, looking at my clothes covered by dirt, and my face intoxicated from propane fumes. A dangerous aftermath ended as a tragedy—but thanks to God, I am alive. A survivor walking on ash around the dead tyrannosaurus. I killed the beast!

In front of me, tall cactuses dominate most of the habitat corridors between the reptile population and terrestrial carnivores. Seeing my surroundings from an unobstructed view, I wonder which direction to take. I guess my next choice will be to follow the ridge.

As a patient man, I go after finding my dream place. My life depends on me proving I have the physical strength to defend myself. Throughout this journey, a survivor's own adaptation to nature helps avoid imminent danger. I head through the ridge where extreme climate change temperatures are difficult to withstand. I should focus on the life skill to safeguard my surroundings and prevent an attack by choosing which path is a better avenue to secure my freedom. I am trapped in the middle of a desert with no survival resources and no companion.

Many miles of walking on hot sand as my feet swell from ripped shoes. I have no umbrella to keep shaded from the sweltering sun. Dark orange skies create an interesting new daylight! I can't find the best resting stop with no wristwatch or compass. I am not afraid. Surrendering a fight is not the way of a brave survivor; one must stay strong and protect oneself from danger by fighting beasts.

Wandering in extreme heat, I find a bed-sized rock and lean on it to rest before tomorrow's long day. My first night, I sleep in isolation. I dream of alien creatures walking towards an open field, seeing a funnel cloud within a desert. The ground shakes and I slip over something pointy. Beneath me, the topsoil cracks, and I'm falling deep into the pit, wider than the circumference of a tornado! I wake up in fear. Nothing happened and everything looks quiet. After this awful dream, I stay awake throughout the night till sunrise. In the meantime, I think, what will be my next decision?

It is morning! The winds whistle through my ears, and my stomach aches from having nothing to eat and I have no drinking water to stop the thirst in my dry mouth. I have sudden weakness and lose my senses and cannot smell what's around me, making my sickness worse. I am left hopeless in a depressing world. The challenge is making it to Las Vegas by foot with no compass. I face a challenging destiny to be ready for the unexpected.

I have no choice to move further. I stand up, feeling the pain over my body. My health is not strong enough for this journey. Wandering with blurred vision across the desert, I'm having sunstroke from intense heat. I realize I am a real idiot having trouble learning new life skills as my false judgement pushed me too far.

Ahead of me, a rock is in the shade and I sit on it, considering my next moves. Still, I cannot picture everything. I remember a story from when I travelled to Yellowstone National Park: I had this crazy idea of sneaking out, walking in the woods with a flashlight on to discover the animal kingdom. My step-father made a campfire with me and I ate s'mores the whole evening and told shocking bedtime stories. An hour later, both of them were in their bed asleep, turning off the lights.

I snuck out with a light on, tip-toeing along a trail, and I bumped into something which made me fall, lying flat on the ground. Most shockingly, I hear a growling bear near me. I screamed for my life. Someone shot the bear!

A group of hunters asked me, "Are you all right, son? Where are your parents? Are you lost?"

I responded, "Yes, sir. They are somewhere not far. I will show you the way."

Accompanied by these male hunters, I was nervous to be punished for running away. Approaching closer to the camp, my step-father came, and I rushed as he pushed me inside the tent.

From my personal learned experiences, I know I should stand my ground if something approaches me. From this moment on, I will protect myself till I reach Las Vegas. I move forward through the shade, heading toward a secret path. I fear any wrong direction is dangerous, a risk that wild animals will follow my footsteps in silent motion for a kill; strangers attack those who wander on quiet land. Since the natural world has interesting wonders, I walk on a hill at high elevation, realizing deserts have shortcuts which lead to death traps.

My journey continues to follow a strange path, and I see no signs of any road or highway. Lost in the middle of a desert surrounded by tall cactuses and the blistering sun makes me lose my vision as I walk in deadly heat. Tired from this constant travel, weak and unable to take a single footstep, I fall, lying on the ground, unconscious, and my eyes close.

Awakening, I don't know how long someone has been splattering my face with water. Around me, a group of indigenous people look at me as they talk amongst themselves in an unfamiliar language. The scariest moment is seeing my skin burned in dark red blisters. Brought as an outsider into their camp, I think, what am I doing here? A shy indigenous leader does not introduce himself. I'm lost, trying to find a way out.

"My name is Joshua. I have no food and no water. I come here in peace." An indigenous leader translates my words from English to their native language. They look at me sentimentally.

He introduces himself, "I am Martin, the chief of this tribe. We are sorry to see you left alone in isolation, and we welcome you to our people. You will eat and be well rested. Later, we will take you on a horse ride." I thank them for their generosity.

The stallion gallops through the desert. Along the way, coyotes migrate on top of the rocky mountains and wolf packs howl in the far east under sizzling temperatures.

I ask, "Martin, how much further?"

"Early tomorrow morning," he predicts.

The day ends with a gorgeous sunset. I sense a change in my body energy as the sun's ultraviolet warmth touches my face. It is nightfall, and the entire tribe camps inside a cave and asks me to join them. I sleep on a rag, leaning my back against a big pointy rock not as comfortable. These tribesmen safeguard me; they create a fireplace from dry shrubs to keep everyone warm throughout this chilly night.

The next morning, we continue across the desert where lizards roam, establishing their nests beside cactuses. Two vultures circle above us, looking for their closest prey. The sun is at twelve o'clock. I look at five tents where these indigenous people live within their own territory, hunting for wild animals. We made it! I jump off the stallion, following the chief, and we walk together towards a tent where his wife will be the one taking care of me till I am rested. After three days being encamped, I'm feeling better. Later, I run to the tribal leader.

Speaking to Martin, I say, "I have seen my health progress and I am ready to go on my route to Las Vegas."

Martin says, "Ok, Joshua. We will leave tomorrow at dawn. Rest!"

The next day, the tribesman prepare the horses for this trip as they will come with me as my companions, protecting me from danger. We gathered enough food supplies, including water and blankets. The entire village supplies bows and arrows to hunt and defend ourselves from unwanted enemies. Leaving the camp, the villagers wave at us for a last goodbye.

On the saddle, my horse gallops fast, like driving in a sports car, and I see the desert mountains from far. The breeze blows through my hair and the hot air makes me sweat as I'm dressed too warm for this climate.

I question Martin, "Have you ever seen a casino?"

Martin replies, "Yes, Joshua. Follow me through these bushes and we will climb to the top, observing an unobstructed view. Later, we move further toward the plain fields."

"Great! Let's do this!" I cheer.

We leave our horses, climbing a cliff to see a magnificent view of Las Vegas, five kilometres away from us. The chief and I stand wondering—how will we descend the mountain? Stepping over big rocks and falling on small stones, we have a rough descent along the steep hill and we jump off a sharp angle at a low elevation. On rough sand, we run fast, reaching Las Vegas. We stroll inside the city and there's no one but us! We walk in the shadows of the abandoned city.

Strolling through the street, we witness the malaise of destruction and dead human bodies along the road. I travel in hell, suffering a dreadful journey, lost in the middle of a desert. Las Vegas has changed into an uncivilized world. My spontaneous vacation is the end of my dream. A massacre of spilled blood. Massive fire rips through the windows of the Bellagio, guns with no ammunition found on the sidewalk and buses burned into ash.

I never felt such a scorcher. Martin and I spot a dazzling reflection on a tall building, which causes our eyes to flicker—blurred vision, seeing nothing. A few minutes later, I know something disastrous will happen, and the skyscraper collapses less than a half-kilometre away! The road shakes! I stand watching, and a tsunami of dust darkens the sky. Martin grabs my hand and we run fast, searching for a good place to seek shelter. Street corners buried under fallen debris. It looks much worse than a snowstorm. We walk on deep rubble and sandy conditions. Rushing inside a building, kicking the washroom door wide open, and Martin locks it. He saved my life!

Sometime later, we take the elevator up to the fortieth floor. Martin sees a helicopter! Planning our travel, I guess Chicago is a wonderful place for us to go. In the helicopter, we are both flying; below, fallen debris blankets Las Vegas into dust!

Chapter 14

Inside Planet Earth's Secret World

Career Life

Professor James Peterson is a historian at the Environmental Institute of Climatology. He does extensive research on Earth. At a climate summit in Copenhagen, Denmark, he took part in a discussion forum by listening to foreign secretaries. Waiting until the meeting ended, he raised the question:

"Are we ready to combat global warming with our lack of funding from corrupt governments?"

The climate summit motivates him to save the planet from global warming and to one day become an environmental activist. Every delegate sitting at their tables is stunned to listen to his knowledge. Everyone applauds. James does a great job leading this discussion.

One evening, James returns home after his long flight from

Denmark. The next day, he goes straight to the dean to introduce his project proposal.

He knocks at the dean's door. "Come in, James."

He says, "Mr. Clifford, I am proposing something fantastic for the faculty: travelling to Brazil. If you allow me to go for a six-month sabbatical, I will bring my research findings over to my master studies students. I count on this opportunity for my dissertation to be approved by the PhD program."

Mr. Clifford says, "Fine. Do you agree to pay for your own travel expenses?" James says ok.

Mr. Clifford says, "Tomorrow will be your first day of sabbatical. I hope your study goes well and good luck."

They shake hands, and James closes the door and leaves the office. This is the most exciting moment of his lifetime; at home he's preparing his belongings throughout the night and booking the trip to Brazil.

The Journey

James has a late afternoon flight. Inside a taxicab, an outspoken driver plays loud music which gives him a headache—not an impressive start to the trip! At the airport, James pays his fare, leaving the taxi behind, and rushes through the entrance doors looking for the check-in—a sign displaying "International Airways." In front, James sees no people, having a strange impression he is the one passenger on this plane! He approaches the ticket counter and presents his passport while waiting for his boarding pass.

He goes through customs with a carry-on suitcase, a duffle bag, and his camera. Takes a short stroll around the lounge section for a place to eat. James needs food before this trip. His stomach grumbled. Notices a coffee shop. He drinks his espresso and eats a small bite of the fruit donut.

The attendant announces: "Boarding will be in fifteen minutes."

James grabs his belongings and other travel documents and sees ten other travellers, much less than expected for an airbus flight. He has a nervous breakdown waiting for the plane to takeoff! Can't find the right section. At an empty spot next to the window by the right wing, James fastened his seatbelt tight, experiencing this anxiety as the airplane moves in slow motion towards the runway! He covers his ears with both hands and makes a deep swallow, his feet shaking from the powerful thrust, making him dizzy with confusion.

It is 7:00 pm, and he's hungry for a quick snack. James sits alone in the aisle. An hour later, a flight attendant announces dinner will be in thirty minutes. Grabs a chocolate donut, but his taste buds are craving a wholesome supper. Inputs his headphones and listens to classical opera and snoozes from the changing musical tones. Something pokes James's left shoulder. Half-waken, he sees a hot meal carried towards him.

Unexpectedly, the airplane descends in dangerous turbulence. James looks through the right window. The engine is in flames! Grabs a ventilator—breathing through it to save himself from suffocation as the airplane spins; broken free from the seatbelt, he runs fast through the main aisles, seeing ten dead passengers lying on the floor, including both pilots. Inside the cabin, no idea how to turn around this plane, James finds no landing spot through the violent storm clouds frequented by lightning bolts and heavy rain.

He glances through the cockpit window to his left, knows his current location is somewhere in the Pacific. With fears of death, James has no choice but to risk his survival by landing this plane in the ocean. Pushing the airplane yoke, he puts this plane in rapid downward motion, and icy water slams through the cockpit windows, James sinking into the depths. He frees himself as he swims upward. Below him, the airplane smashes into the coral reefs and explodes in flames. Later, James spots of a life jacket drifting by in monstrous waves.

It is morning. Awakened under the scorching sun on the ocean, James is lost on open sea. The deadly climate is overwhelming for him. For days and nights, James floats many long miles, having strange dreams after the plane crush. James becomes desperate from starvation.

Large tidal waves kept on dragging James in unstable directions. Seasick from drinking salty water on an emptied stomach, his loss of appetite worsens each day. It has been twenty days lost on open seas and there's no sign of any approaching ship and no island. Without food, it will be difficult to survive. James has a life jacket on but is in danger of being eaten by ferocious man-eating sharks—search for blood, surfacing in the murky water.

With no compass and no map, James's hopelessness shatters his soul. James floats half-naked with a stiffened back, heart-broken, and cannot sleep in his stripped clothes. A desperate survivor struggling to find directions. It has been a month of this unpredictable journey, since the plane crash and for thousands of miles, James starves. James sees no rescue ship! Praying each day, he wishes to be on an island soon, not on water.

If someone had found James, by now he would have completed his project! He knows living within a dystopian world is one tragedy after another. Survivors should never abandon their destiny. As a teacher with no survival experience, he cannot imagine this difficult misfortune, as his journey continues to be challenging. Tired of floating with a life jacket on in stormy seas. James is taken to unknown places by tidal waves.

The Amazon Rainforest

James hears a waterfall, panicking, with no chance to reverse. Drops in midair from a height higher than an eleven-storey building. Below, James notices many unusual species which he's never seen. Falls on his back into a marsh, stands on both feet, throwing his life jacket away—looks at himself, naked in humiliation with no spare clothes. In this rainforest, James faces a strange world. He wonders what happened to nature?

His complexion is ridiculous without anything to wear. Before moving further towards danger to explore the animal kingdom, James will use palm leaves to create clothing. Defenceless and worried his fresh clothes will attract jungle predators, he walks on conifers, having a pain in both legs as slippery rocks cause his feet to swell. He's trapped inside the Amazonian rainforest; the place known to be Brazil. James descends into the jungle, where he will adapt, his camouflage protecting him from invasive predators. After a few hours strolling with no rest stop, James hears the almighty roars. A tiger rages in his direction. James can't die. Bumps into a tall palm tree, hitting himself hard, and falls on thick sludge, dizzy. Wakes up noticing his dirty body as blood drips from his forehead. He has nothing to use as a patch. Runs fast through the conifers, looking for the hillside.

A boiling and steamy evening, the skies turn into strange colours, which gives James an odd impression of a tropical storm. With no idea where else to go, he makes camp from bamboo logs and palm leaves; out of nowhere, James hears somebody coming to the rescue. Looks around and notices from afar a group of soldiers jumping from their chopper looking for James, and he runs straight towards them. They grab him by the arm and tranquilize him—he faints.

James wakes up on a hospital bed, sees his friends bringing gift baskets over to him. Undergoes painful procedures on his paralyzed feet, and stomach surgery. For days, James cries in his bed about not completing his research study. He is an environmentalist who became a teacher and turned into a brave survivor. A striking story. Two weeks later, James returns to school to conduct a short seminar.

A participant questions, "Mr. Peterson, are you saying our planet is in peril of climate change?"

James points out, "Yes. Extreme temperatures will lead to dangerous weather." Quizzing the class, he asks, "What will climate change do to us?"

He concludes, "In the end, heavy pollutants will affect the ozone hole layer. We do not realize how Earth will be throughout the twenty-first century." Everyone applauds.

After the presentation, James is proud of his achievement; he's engaged himself to do extensive research on Planet Earth. Not tired of answering more questions, James has new ideas come to mind while talking. It is late afternoon, and students are returning to their classes—the perfect timing for a coffee break? James leaves the auditorium, thanking the audience for their participation. Goes out for a walk.

Having been away for more than a year, James sees the school has changed. He sees new tall buildings and a vast library nearby! Walking on student grounds, he finds an indoor cafeteria; inside, he sees takeout restaurants and decides where to have lunch. No coffee shop. He wanders around browsing each restaurant and has trouble figuring out what to order. He feels hungry after staring at most of the delicious foods.

Instead of having a cappuccino, James reads through the Greek menu and orders chicken souvlaki. After ordering, he searches for a place to eat within this crowded school cafeteria and finds a brilliant spot beside the window.

Ready to eat lunch, James closes his eyes, tastes the meat. The spices make him hungrier and he grabs another order. He still remembers the times before he left for his journey. James has survived the biggest and toughest challenge throughout his lifetime, learned to never stop what you are doing. After eating, he sits, reading his memoir written from the trip. Sees the illegible writing on wavy pages after his book sunk into the ocean, which made James upset—his work unpublished!

James leaves the cafeteria. Outside, he meets Phil Rodrick, a political science professor. They greet each other. Chatting outside, James talks about his experiences from the trip and what he has learned of being a lost survivor. Dreadful memories make it emotional for James remembering the plane crash and he thinks that everything happened because of climate change. Phil is stunned to hear James's long story! But, there's more! James concludes his story when he shares an interesting moment when he was drifted away not on the ocean currents, but on a sea mammal—unknown—which saved his life. When Phil heard this, he's silenced, thinking that James is lying. In the end, Phil speaks the truth: his secret that he called a close friend in the U.S. Army who rescued James from the Amazon. James gives thanks to Phil for being trustworthy and concerned.

Chapter 15

Lost Island

I was born on December 12, 1990. My parents named me Napoleon, a unique name for a masculine child brought into this world of exploration. As a few-month-old baby, I read pirate books—flipping from page to page, looking at original paintings of the open sea, which gave me adventurous dreams.

As a five-year-old, on a gorgeous afternoon, I was with my parents at the Toronto Harbourfront, where ships sailed near the waterfront and stopped beside the pier. On the cruise ship sailing across Lake Ontario, we sat and ate seafood. The bell rang. Inside the cabin, my father raised me to take the helm and in front of me I saw a massive bowsprit facing the Toronto Islands. Walking through the dining section, someone approached us. "May I look at your boarding passes, please," commands Captain Nick-Francis.

I hear Nick's set-sail announcement. "We'll be cruising along the waterfront near the CNE. Enjoy!!"

Captain Nick gave every person hats, except me. There were no hats left! My dad gave me his instead. After a full hour of cruising, we entered the gates of Polson Pier—a brilliant spot to take magnificent photos. Returning home after this trip, I drew sketches all night long and wrote this poem.

What a lovely day we are having!

Today, we have great wind currents and no sign of rain.

We are set-sailing towards our destination, and the scorching heat makes our heads swelter from humidity.

At school, daydreaming to be in training at cadet school and learning to navigate a ship. I enjoyed presenting myself in front of others to show my genuine passions. One time after school, my parents came to pick me up, and in the car, I interrupted their conversation.

"I want to be enrolled as a recruit for summer camp—"

My mother said, "No, son, you are too young to be a cadet."

After this talk, I knew my father did not consider my idea. In grade three, every Friday, Ms. Kathy gave a full day off from studying to take a trip to a museum somewhere in the city. Inside the museum, touring with the entire group, I glanced at remarkable paintings of battle ships; seeing artistic images intrigued me. Leaving myself behind gave me freedom and the chance to explore. I tripped over something and fell inside a big ship and my classmate stood on deck, pretending to be real pirates lost at sea. Climbing a ladder, I found wooden rum casks, a helm, and a golden bell.

Ms. Kathy yelled to me daydreaming on deck, "Napoleon, where are you!?"

I jumped off, injuring myself, not knowing the height of this ship. I was in such pain when the school principal grabbed my arm as I cried while strolling. Displeased my parents. The fantasy world troubles me when I experience crazy dreams of sailing across the ocean. Coming home from school, my parents are angry at me; from now on, I will forget cadet school.

On a late Sunday evening before sleep, I speak with my mother: "I wish to sail enrolling myself in the summer program."

Mom reacts, "Son, lost at sea is dangerous, where Earth's powerful force is robust and vicious in its overall environment."

I argue, "You don't know the stormy seas since you are afraid of water."

She raises her voice. "This is not true! Have a goodnight's rest before tomorrow's class!"

Miss Gruenwald, the school principal, she organized the performance date before convocation. Acting alone in my room, preparing my play script for the upcoming stage performance. This is my moment to prove to my parents that I am fit to be a recruit.

Miss Gruenwald speaks to me, "How do you call yourself?"

Raising my hand high, I say, "My name is Napoleon. I want to act as a sailor stranded on an island."

Today is my day for showing an impressive performance where Mom and Dad will take brilliant pictures of me acting on stage. Backstage, I rehearse my role several times in my sailor's costume before the Master of Ceremonies announces my name. Anxious, my first time on stage facing a wider audience. A beam of flashing light illuminates the wide auditorium. The projector displays an image of a pirate ship, and I act as a sailor washed ashore. I wait for a rescue ship to take me back to America.

"I need a cadet," announces a handsome captain dressed in a blue outfit.

I reach out. "Take me."

The captain responds, "What is your nickname, young man?"

I introduce myself. "I am Napoleon."

On stage, I look confused, seeing no crew onboard, and the commander grabs my arms with fierce intent, staring at me as if I were his slave. I grab a broom, washing the deck, and out of nowhere a pirate ship enters, firing a cannonball from a close distance! The drama stops when I kick the cabin door wide open and free everyone jumping into frigid water.

After the play, I listen to the entire audience applauding and whistling because they enjoyed the show. The principal greets everyone and thanks the performers for their drama. I see Mom and Dad walking along the staircase, stunned by my act.

"Son, we will enroll you in cadet school next month," my parents say.

I hug them. "Thank you!"

Someone calls out, "You are a great actor, Napoleon." I am proud of myself.

A week passes. My schoolteacher, Mr. Davidson, will take everyone for a long excursion on a sailboat—five to ten kilometres away from Port Credit near Hamilton, preparing us for a short trip! On a kayak, my instructor gives us each a fishing rod and lectures on how to use it. We have snorkelling equipment to learn to swim.

Mr. Davidson lectures, "Do you feel the energy of the environment?"

He shouts on the count of one, two, three!! I dive into the grey murky lake. Something happens. I spot someone drowning ten metres away, and I swim fast, grabbing an arm towards the yacht.

"I need help!!" I panic. In front of me, my coach performs CPR. Good news, the person recovers!

Mr. Davidson says, "Napoleon, you have proven your impressive skills for becoming a sailor. Do you wish to sail the Atlantic?"

I respond, "I am honoured!"

He announces, "You will leave next week on June 25. Prepare yourself, and we'll meet at Pearson International for our flight to St. John and upon arrival, other recruits will go with us."

The luckiest day of my life; always dreaming of being alone at open sea. I'm nervous to mention to Mom and Dad that I want to leave for the Atlantic Coast.

Coming home, I speak, "Mr. Davidson proposed me heading to St. John for two months, where I will learn as a professional sailor cadet with much older cadets."

My mother is in tears, and my father is heartbroken. I lie on my bed, awake throughout the night, having fears of tomorrow. This is the day, June 25, 2008, 7:30 am—preparing the luggage in my room. I have no choice but to leave my toys behind and my cat, too, as I'm afraid of being teased by other cadets. Closing up my room, I go downstairs and at the front door my cat comes to me— meowing—and I cuddle her.

Dad hands me his canoeing Olympic medal from Russia and puts it around my neck. "This is yours. Come back with it."

In the car, I call Mr. Davidson. "I am leaving for Pearson International Airport with my parents."

When we arrive at Terminal 3, my teacher is sitting at a coffee shop and he greets Mom and Dad with a warm welcome. He speaks of last week's lifesaving moment, during which I proved I have talents to become a professional sailor. There's an hour left till my flight to St. John, and with my teacher, we go to the ticket counter to gather our boarding passes. I see Mom and Dad's faces blushed in tears, making me cry. Together, we go ahead to the Customs Section where I hug them for the last time—not knowing when I'll return home. I wave goodbye.

When we land in St. John we find the sailor cadets waiting at the Arrivals—we meet them, their names: Tom and Charles. On the half-hour-long ride towards the seaboard, I see the fisheries and many seagulls. Arriving at a hotel, I open the car door, and the breezy air smells like raw salmon. I see a large ship called the *Large Swan*. This time, looking inside the ship fascinates me. I spend the night at the inn.

The next morning, I smell something tasty from downstairs and find ten sailors eating their delicious breakfast. I join them in silence. An hour passes. We take our belongings to the reception desk, ready for checkout. Outside, the paparazzi approach us, taking pictures as we're about to set-sail. No time for photographs. Everyone goes up the stairwell towards deck. The masts are set up. My responsibility is to steer the helm in a counter-clockwise direction until the bowsprit faces the ocean. Eight hours have passed since the departure from St. John, and I am the one in charge.

Captain John Afflock approaches me. "Take a break, mate."

I respond, "Thank you, sir. I will be here writing my first poem, 'Long Time At Sea.'"

Above me, massive white sails whistle in the light wind. Glance at the Atlantic Ocean, hear dolphins squeaking as their Creator's voice.

Listening to the ship's bell ringing in commemoration of the last time I looked at my parents as tears filled my eyes. Grief-stricken.

No food, shivering in the fog, and a good bottle of rum will remedy.

Ocean currents wrestle as my ship sailing in murky waters.

I see a full moon behind me across the dark skies. Back home, the weather is quiet.

Sound asleep, hearing my roommates snore.

I creating this composition for an hour; my first evening on a ship makes me depressed about not seeing my parents anymore. The ship heads farther towards deeper waters. It is around midnight; everyone is starving. Many hours with no bread as our stomachs grumbled louder than the ship cruising.

Napoleon says, "Where is the foodstuff?"

Captain Afflock says, "These fools stole everything to celebrate with their feast without inviting us."

A roommate shouts, "I found rum! Who wants to drink?"

Not in the mood for drinking, I write another short lyric before bedtime instead of joining them. Half-wake, I feel the ship rambling from side to side and my window is slammed by tons of ocean water leaking beneath the wooden floor. Rushing onto the main deck dressed in my pyjamas, the ship detaches! Looking for Captain Afflock; I found him dead and saw his entire body paralyzed from starfish.

Myself, I am the one person alive. The others are dead. I have no idea where I am, and the weather turns deadly as strong winds blown the masts away, shaking the yardarm which falls, splitting the main deck apart. I'm alone with no help when the ship sinks into frigid water. In front of the bowsprit, a large whirlpool forms at a close distance! Desperate. I wear no life jacket and grasp onto the handrails. The ship spins 'round and 'round as I jump into the sea, swimming my best through monstrous waves. I hit a rock!

A few hours later, I see daylight as I wake up on a sandy shoreline under the tropical sun. Washed ashore on a deserted island somewhere in the Caribbean—finding myself stranded on the coast where desolation is a matter of survival. Hunting for wild animals is my military tactic to feed myself. My fears of what I will eat beware me of rare and endangered species which could be poisonous, putting my life at risk.

I'm stuck on this island with no help. Unpredictable climate scenarios might change for the worst; escape is too dangerous when strong winds produce a large tide. I go to the shipwreck to collect the goods for building my fortress, gathering the ammunition, including the gunpowder. I find other foods and stock up the alcohol.

Bringing my supplies on a small raft, I prepare for the unexpected. As a survivor, I use wood to build my tent, find a conch to alert anyone, and make a wooden spear to kill wild animals. The killing of innocent species destroys my connection with God. I will force myself to work each day with hard labour by avoiding rest on the Sabbath.

My first night, the day of my arrival, I have a frightening dream of a massive colony invading my camp. Awakening the next morning, I look around, seeing a strange world of half-human savages leaving a trail of destruction where the remains of Native warriors are swept away by tidal waves. I walk along the shoreline seeing nasty beast footprints on red sand; the winds whistle through my ears and the mist evaporates from the ocean.

I make a fast return to my tent, and my clothes are stripped into pieces. It looks shocking. My camp has been destroyed by something unknown. Leaving my camp behind, I head east towards a palm tree—hiding behind the rocks, I look at an enormous house where a half-human animal beast crawls across the garden. A biological experiment to destroy this planet.

With my spear, gun, and hunting knife—I try to keep a close eye out for my surrounding enemies. Positioning myself at high latitude, facing the sea, I have a fantastic view and feel the cool ocean breeze but no sunshine. Isolated on top of a mountain with no people and weird weather. Misfortune is compromising my survival.

On the second morning, I wander, looking for food. I see dead organisms bitten at every corner as blood spreads from their bodies. I find myself lost in the middle of nowhere. Resting on the ground, awakened, creepy sounds echo near me. I stand up under long, loose tree branches, feeling the pain inside my lungs from the sweltering heat. Dizzy, I run back to my fortress.

If I stay strong, I have a better chance of overcoming loneliness. Intuition is one of my strengths gained from cadet school. I remember when I saved the person from drowning; survivors never abandon others, and my secret is God will guide you wherever place you choose to go. Nature brings sustenance to life if humans respect it. Hiding behind the bush to see the enemy as a perfect spot for camouflage. I am a survivor who is not afraid of anyone. I have the power to stop the evil against humankind. Am I the last person to end this massacre?

For six hours straight, looking through the bush, I suspect monsters roam over the shoreline in a dangerous position to attack anyone alive, which includes me—stranded and nervous. If I am captured, I will either face ugliness or save myself with dignity. I have two choices: build a raft to escape or stay deserted. The island turns much worse; I jump out, finding myself surrounded by beasts. The remains of dead flesh lie on the charcoal shoreline. I never saw such disturbing imagery.

Touching the black sand with my bare hands, I hear strange sounds behind me. A pack of half-human beasts storm towards me. I am caught in daylight and surrounded by ugly-looking creatures hungry for a kill! They hit me on the head with something heavy and I fall on the ground, unconscious.

I have a weird impression I'm locked inside a patient's room, my wrists and legs in heavy chains. Someone brought me here as a vagrant. Inside the inhumane chamber of scientific madness, I notice the genetic cloning of mortal bodies vivisected for a biological experiment. Through the glass window, I see an evil doctor approaching me, carrying a kit. Am I going to die?

He stares at me with his red eyes. "My name is Dr. Brunsmirg and I am the director of this institute."

I burst, "What do you want?"

Dr. Brunsmirg grabs me, screaming, "This island is mine! I will turn every alive human into an animal, including you! My world is no freedom, destruction is my true blood, putting Earth on its knees much sooner than you think!"

He pushes me inside a laboratory chamber. Inside the surgery suite, I have no chance for last-minute prayers! Someone injects me with a sedative as I lie on the bed undergoing surgery. Feeling a deep cut, pierced through my scalp. I have undergone a brain transplant.

Later, I wake up in the surgery room staring around in a nightmarish shock, seeing my long, hairy arms and my skinny, bent legs. I glance at the mirror, watching as my face turns into a werewolf's. Inflicted with a deadly disease from vermin. It looks much worse than euthanasia.

I say to myself, "Dr. Brunsmirg is a monster! Think, Napoleon, can I stop him from destroying the world?"

The door is open, and it's my last chance to take revenge and save myself from torture by escaping the evil Dr. Brunsmirg. I break free, running through the narrow corridor, where I hear the brutal suffering of animals undergoing a cloning experiment when RNA and DNA are both paired.

On the wall, I find an alarm switch and pull it, and the beasts storm through the narrow corridor, breaking doors and shattering windows. Looking for the nearest exit, I notice Dr. Brunsmirg holding a pistol in his right hand—staring at me in the real mood for a fight. I rage with a powerful punch, hitting him hard, and he flies across the corridor where he lies on the floor, bleeding. I grab his pistol, shooting him in the head twice to avenge the others.

Outside, I find an unused needle. I decide to take a life risk by injecting myself with this vaccine, hoping it will save me, changing me into an actual human, back to the old Napoleon. I notice my limbs returning to normal! Excited to be cured as a free man—alive and healthy.

Above me, I see cyclonic skies forming beyond a twenty-storey tsunami! The tidal waves strike, and the laboratory explodes into flames. This is God's retribution to punish evil insanity. The tsunami makes landfall, and I am swept away, taking a deep breath. Palm trees sink with beasts drowned. A miracle has happened. I swim, using my physical strength to rescue myself from dark water. The next morning, I wake up, seeing my island has transformed! God's power did this for me, abolishing the unnatural. I wonder, will I ever return home?

On the shoreline, I see no palm trees—emptiness! This deserted setting shocks me! I must decide whether to wait here till a rescue ship comes, or risk swimming in deep water. Cadet school trained me to survive as a real sailor in history, in those tough moments. My teacher told me to be calm and never abandon your place if you're not ready to move forward.

I sit on the sand, remembering my home. I wander the shoreline, angry; I did not listen to my mother. I learned never to go on an expedition alone! I should have listened to her before attempting this challenge. I have been naïve, wanted to become a professional sailor, failed.

I am stranded on the island for fourteen days with no food on an empty stomach; on the fifteenth morning, out of nowhere, a rescue ship blows its horns. I wave, jumping, calling out, "Wait!!" I swim fast into deep water; in front of me, two divers in blue life jackets swim towards me and they grab me by the arms. Minutes later, I am aboard a rescue ship safe and sound, ready to return home!

I sit on deck exhausted, not hungry after being stranded as a brave survivor. I fought dangerous villains with a strong heart. I have double vision and am feeling seasick. Someone brings me food and I fall asleep on deck. On stormy seas, I sleep for days and my appetite is low from starvation!

A few more days pass and I wake up on the ship well-rested! Staring at myself in the mirror, I see I've lost weight. I'm too weak to be a sailor. Given plenty of food inside my cabin, I eat and have more energy.

Four weeks cruising on the Atlantic Coast, seeing pleasant weather and no rainstorm. The ship sails north towards Charlotte-town, the capital of Prince Edward Island, which will be my last stop! Before nightfall, I arrive and prepare for a flight from Charlottetown Airport to Toronto. I can't wait till the moment I meet my parents at the door!

On the plane, I fall asleep, dreaming. My parents moved elsewhere! This wakes me. The propeller plane makes a complete stop! It is morning, cloudy and rainy.

I have no phone with me, forgotten my home, cannot remember my real name, and I experience trouble going through customs with no passport, but I make it! I sit trying to remember my real name; spent one night at the airport. Something comes to mind.

My name is Napoleon Jr. Smith! I run into a police officer named Sergeant Peter Williams.

Sergeant Williams asks me, "What is your name, sir?"

"Napoleon Smith," I said.

"Where are your parents?"

"I don't know?"

He looks at the computer and finds their location.

"Follow me to my squad car and I will drive you. Come!"

Inside his car, he drives fast on the 427 Highway, honking at traffic for a steady ride. After a thirty-minute drive from the airport, I am riding through a small neighbourhood of semi-detached houses. Our last stop. He escorts me to a nearby house and knocks on the door a few times, and it opens! Mom is standing at the door!

I look into my mother's eyes. She has changed since I left my parents. She hugs me, seeing the "new" Napoleon. I've never felt such care and compassion after days of struggles. My mother takes my hand, bringing me into the living room to reunite with my father. I look around in surprise at my home—elegant and spacey! My dad is lying on his recliner reading a newspaper and does not react to my mother's voice.

She speaks aloud, "Napoleon is our son. He loves you!"

No word. I don't know why my father does not want to talk to me, ignoring my presence and paying no attention. I made a mistake coming back. Is a shame if I leave?

Tired of standing, waiting for my father to speak, Mom shows me to my room. I walk inside; it's tidy everywhere! I undress myself, and she looks at me in shock. I lost a ton of weight. Pretending to fall asleep, I hear her cry. Lying on the right side of my bed, I face the wall. Hours pass; I sleep dreaming of nothing, a good sign, no awakening with nightmares. I wake up seeing my dad coming to me dressed in his old sleeping gown.

He touches my back and whispers, "Good morning, my son. Have you slept well?"

I yawn. "Yes, Dad."

He speaks, "Come, let's have breakfast."

Sitting at the dinner table in my pyjamas, saying no word. I eat delicious food. My cat joins me to keep close company. My father asks me to tell the story of my long journey. My mother hears me speak as a talented storyteller.

Chapter 16

The Natural Disaster
of April 7, 2042

On **April 7, 2042**, Alex wakes up at 7:00 am to catch the school bus, seeing his parents leave for work. No time to prepare breakfast. Trained himself to be self-organized, doing everything as a mature adult. His parents didn't bring him up as an adult.

The school bus stops beside his house. Alex, dressed in his day-to-day uniform, tying his shoes at the door, looks at his ordinary wristwatch. Runs fast to board, seeing his best friends from math class, Laura and Timothy.

Alex sits with them at the far end, their favourite spot. It's fun to bounce up on the seat when the school bus runs over a pothole. Looking through the window, opening it for fresh air. Sunshine, a gorgeous day for recess. A shame to attend class and miss the fun, especially when listening to the math teacher, Mr. Walter, lecturing everyone on geometry.

Alex did not bother looking through yesterday's homework, knowing he will have a poor grade on his upcoming report card. Loves reading books and writing stories, but is a low-average student in junior high. In room 214, Mr. Walter locks the backdoor and asks everyone to show him their math assignment from yesterday. Alex looks through his homework, worries his answers might be wrong. His hands shake and forehead sweats, blushed.

Mr. Walter announces, "The class will begin in five minutes."

He stands right next to Alex's desk. "May I see your homework?"

Alex gives Mr. Walter the assignment, and he grabs and grades it! Is ready to give it back. Alex looks at many red markings, noticing a failing grade! Disappointed! Stares at the smiley faces for those who had done well. It makes him angry as a terrible student!

This is not Alex's day! When Mr. Walter turns his back to him, Alex runs to another desk to sit behind the class, hoping Mr. Walter does not suspect him of hiding from his lesson. Grabbing his textbooks, putting them on the desk, Alex looks through equations and problem-solving questions, different from the take-home assignments. He cannot wait to have lunch but it is only 10:00 am and still two hours remain till lunchtime. The difficulties of learning math with no motive in strategic thinking shake Alex. He takes notes while listening to Mr. Walter teaching the class trigonometry, a smart approach to prepare for the next assignment.

With an hour left, Mr. Walter calls Susanna to come up, allowing her to teach trigonometry to the class. She stands up, speaking, having done her homework. Alex sits ashamed of himself. He is not smart enough. For fifteen minutes, till the class ends, he rests and doesn't bother writing notes. It looks like he'll give up and not pass the test. He's relaxed, not worrying his dad will slap him in the face.

Class ends, and Alex is on a lunch break, taking his peanut butter jelly sandwich and chocolate milk from the lunchbox, a no-vitamin meal. Going to the main cafeteria, exhausted after the hard math lesson, he's relieved to take a seat alone and have a quiet space for eating lunch. He doesn't see Laura and Timothy. It looks as they are both absent. Exhausted. Alex did not want to miss his upcoming English class with Ms. Julie Tompkins—an outstanding teacher who always appreciates hard work, not like Mr. Walter.

Suddenly, the tables shakes, and everyone slides away! The others scream. Panicking teachers rush to the lunchroom, helping everyone to stay calm, hoping the fire department will come. The walls crumble and the floors split. The soccer field erodes, and the weather still looks nice. Alex hurries to warn everyone.

He calls out, "We are experiencing an earthquake! We must stay for our lives' sakes!"

Wanders across the hallway. Classes are empty, and the glass shattered on the floor. No one to ask for help. Someone is lying on the ground, hurt. Alex approaches, recognizing him as Thomas, Timothy's younger brother!

He whispers to Thomas, "Are you all right?"

Thomas speaks in a quavering voice, "Thanks, Alex." Alex carries him, heading back to the cafeteria to reach out for help.

He brings Thomas to his gym teacher, Mr. Adams. "You are a brave man!"

Within the hallway, he's searching for anyone lost or hurt; the damage is terrible! Alex finds his guidance counsellor, Ms. Peterson, and the school principal, Mr. McDonald—both dead! Runs back, frightened.

Alarming everyone, he says, "Mr. McDonald will not be with us." Everyone cries.

Again, leaving the school cafeteria, Alex walks towards the gymnasium, opens the door, peaks inside the flooded gym! In shock. He did not expect this impact. Curious, he goes up the staircase to the second floor, searching for others. Upstairs, in the empty hallway, textbooks are underwater! Every classroom door opens; Alex's heartbeat pounds fast as he steps on the wet floor. He hears nothing. Out of nowhere, rats crawl everywhere! Hides himself in the boy's washroom.

Alex's wristwatch shows it's 1:00 pm, passed lunch break. In his old sneakers, he opens the door and walks across the hallway. The flood is everywhere! Jumps inside Mr. Andrews' science classroom, picking up the phone, dialling 9-1-1. The phone line is dead! Alex finds an old computer in the library, turns it on, and emails his parents. No internet connection!

No cellphones. Alex has no other choice but to return to the school cafeteria. Leaves the room and runs downstairs to save his classmates and teachers, his old sneakers soaked from stinky toilet water, which gives him the chills.

Alex suspects teachers leading their students out of the gym. Cockroaches are everywhere! How will he pass through this place? Running, he makes it, managing well for his age.

He calls out, "My name is Alex!"

His French teacher Madame Fortune orders him, "Please stay with the group!"

He follows the classmates, heading for the parking lot through the massive doors. Unexpectedly, water moves fast through our legs where the lockers fall apart. Everyone holds hands, trying to make it through the flooding. Freddy, our youngest classmate, lost! Alex goes back to save Freddy's life, forcing himself to put most of his strength into going through the main corridor, seeing water at high levels. Glances, and finds Freddy rushing to him. Alex grabs Freddy's right hand before it's too late, leaning him on his back, feeling his body weight, making small steps as the water rises much worse.

Alex screams, "Can somebody please help me!"

Keeps going. He hears no one; it looks as if they are both trapped in this natural disaster. Unlucky. A wise decision to go forward towards the two doors facing them.

The water is deeper and they are being drowned by the powerful force of rapid currents! Heavy objects are swimming below: textbooks, backpacks, pencils, and lunchboxes. Nothing to hold!

Trouble breathing, Alex swims and bumps Freddy into an entrance door, hitting his forehead hard! Someone comes to their rescue. They are under a lake; the school is sinking! With no life vest, Alex finds a backpack and straps it around Freddy's shoulders to save his life. Alex swims upward, grabs Freddy's left arm, and they make it! Outside, the houses float on rough water and vehicles are swept away by the powerful waves! Are the others dead?

To his right, a house drifts straight towards them. This is their last chance to save Freddy's life, proving Alex is a brave rescuer. They duck, grabbing the rope, and Alex puts Freddy on his back. Helps Freddy to lie on the concrete, performing CPR. Thank God, he's alive!

Freddy questions Alex, "Where am I?"

Alex responds, "Freddy, you are safe with me. I am a grade nine student at our school. Many have gone missing! It looks we are the last ones alive."

They go through the back doors of a detached house, seeing sofas and lamps float on water. Freddy notices a stairwell, and they take it to the rooftop to avoid being drowned. Alex follows him as they share hands, and the ceiling crumbles and they move fast through fallen debris and dust. Their eyes are dry from the allergic sand particles blowing at their faces.

They find a long ladder and they climb it, breaking through the wooden wall, observing the entire neighbourhood destroyed by this giant tsunami sweeping them through trees! They take cover! Holding tight to the balcony rail, scared of what's happening.

The house hits a sturdy bridge, and they fall into the water, trying to swim, dragging themselves from the fast-moving currents, holding tight with both hands onto the metal frame. They make it on solid ground! In exhaustion, they sleep. Waking up, below, they see the calm river flow at a high level!

Alex reassures Freddy, who is heartbroken in tears. "We will follow the road heading north wherever it leads us. Don't worry, I am with you and I will protect you as my younger brother."

They stand up, preparing themselves for a distant journey up north. Flooding is everywhere. It will be a challenge for them to by-pass this reservoir in bare feet. Concerned Freddy might not make it, Alex knows it's his responsibility to guide Freddy along the way. He is much younger, with less experience.

Alex explains to Freddy, "We're not going this way. We will move further towards the lower area where we will pass through the flood. Do you understand?"

Freddy answers, "Yes, Alex."

They carry forward in the southern direction, having a better chance of staying alive. Alex is to keep Freddy safe and bring him home to his parents. This will be a challenge. They pass over the detached bridge straight towards a sign which reads "Private Property." Alex glances around, seeing a barbed wire fence blockading them at every corner, and worse, vicious bulldogs bark at them! Again, running back to the bridge, terrified! No other direction to follow. North or south? They don't know what to expect if they take the wrong path.

Freddy calms Alex. "You are my hero who saved my life. Please, don't quit. Are we in this together?"

Alex points with his right hand. "Yes. We will move west. Freddy, please stay close."

Lots of mud and the fallen debris under the bridge. The impact of this natural disaster on a school day has caused enough trouble for both of them, putting their lives at risk if they don't move. Guessing possible directions with no map or compass, they cannot imagine the dangers they'll face later on when life becomes hectic. Their last choice is to walk on the muddy path heading west. They lost their shoes and their wet feet make us trip over, falling on their backs in dirt, desperate from weakness.

Heading towards an uneven path of large rocks and junk, they walk, monitoring their whereabouts. Beyond the horizon, a flooded landscape and no light where the dark sky gives them a terrible impression a storm might appear. With no clue where they are headed, Alex is worried.

They're on a brave journey, fighting for survival, not afraid to take risks on the verge of death. From this moment on, Alex knows he must pay attention to the dangers of unexpected weather and ferocious land creatures. Defending themselves from present danger is going to be hard, as they continued to move farther on the muddy trail, watching what they step on, noticing body remains buried under deep soil, seeing skeletons everywhere.

Freddy says, "Alex, are we walking in a graveyard?"

The farther they go, the more Freddy suspects the bloody water is the poison from the underworld! This is a sign they are facing the worst beginning of an unimaginable dystopia. Will their lives end? Freddy sees nothing but destruction, a dead ecosystem with no live animals! Terrible to watch nature fall into the pit of climate change. Two brave survivors surviving Earth's worst natural disaster! Still much to figure out. Not knowing how this ends, they are both hopeful. While walking, something drops out from Alex's side pocket—an egg salad sandwich! An uneaten leftover snack.

Alex shouts, "Freddy, I found food!"

Alex feels the sandwich melting in his hands! The fiery-red skies made the sun invisible. They are being watched by the alien universe! Freddy and Alex are in the shadows of death, fighting for survival. Freddy thinks they are ready for the next disaster if it happens.

This weird and tricky path is leading them in a straight direction to nowhere. They follow the same path. Cannot afford any mistakes throughout their mission to a safe return home. They are prepared to stay hungry and are both ready to look after themselves within the alienated and violent planet of natural disasters where the ugly might happen. The last two survivors, scared of Mother Nature's power to destroy the human population. They are strolling on this inhabitant land under a dark orange sky. No groundwater!

Saying no words, they wander within the silence of a dead Planet Earth. Talking aloud will echo their voices—different soundscapes which their enemies might hear from a mile. They don't want any trouble. They search for a hiding spot.

After the tsunami struck, Earth is a dry planet. Alex is the one to protect Freddy on a long and dangerous journey. Being the oldest survivor, he's responsible for saving the life of a young boy too weak to fight outsiders. In silence, they wander in misery, seeing the wreckage of human civilization. What has climate change done to the world? Earth's dark world is no place for inexperienced survivors. To survive, they must take every step to protect themselves from death by risking their lives to continue towards the same muddy path. No shortcuts!

Alex can't tell the time within the arid environment, is shocked to witness the devastating biodiversity loss. This present setting looks much worse than being lost in the wilderness! Nothing flies above them; they hear no bird or live animal. Alex thinks, climate change will harm us in decades to come. How far will I be able to take Freddy further west?

Freddy falls to the ground in weakness after Alex sees him carrying a backpack over skinny shoulders. He carries Freddy, speed walking to save him and search for water. Tearful, seeing drought everywhere! Powerless, with no choices.

His legs ached, but this does not stop him from moving further. No energy to save Freddy's life! Only dry soil on Alex's hands to feed a dying boy. A minute later, Freddy passes out in his arms! Alex cries, shaking him a few times. Freddy is unconscious! He lies dead on Alex's lap! Leaves Freddy behind lying on the ground in his stripped school clothes.

Where is Alex headed? His bare feet swell from tiptoeing on hot rocks, and he bursts in agony! No other choice but not to stop. Picks up the pace. No chance of having a quick break. Alex finds no hiding spot to sleep. Fears he won't last long on an empty stomach in dehydration. A young survivor strolling across the deserted landscape. His surroundings show no sign of hope, and he will find no one alive.

The tsunami has left a trail of destruction and he knows the land mammals migrated somewhere and birds, too. With nothing to feed on, the new era of extinction has started! Alex is unsure where he's walking, his mind is blowing! Remembers Freddy. It makes Alex emotional as the person who tried to take care of him. It is his turn to protect himself and fight for survival till the end of time!

Saddened, Alex stops and sits on the ground, falling fast asleep. A few hours later, he wakes up seeing himself trapped in a dark heavy smog, breathing the dry air, which makes him sweat and his skin tickle. Panics in confusion, running away to escape terror. Not looking back, Alex runs towards a straight path through thick smog, and feels invisible!

Dizzy from trouble breathing, no air in his lungs, coughing, Alex does not stop. Light from a far distance! Watching every step to avoid tripping. The blood from his bare feet bleeds through toenails. Alex screams in pain, feeling the tiny rocks cut through skin.

Above, the smog dissipates and the sky changes colour to turquoise, giving him the power to run longer distances. The breeze comes from the southwest corner, where Alex sees the sun appearing behind the dense smog. A good sign for finding his way back home along a safe path. Notices improvements.

Alex feels the weather pattern might change. The winds gust and temperatures increase. Strong radiation blurs his eyes. His stomach grumbles louder. Nothing will stop him from quitting. Does not know how far he travelled. Remembers the time in science class when Mr. Brown lectured, "If you're lost, follow the sun."

He might be right. At least Alex has learned something. His eyes are wide open as he approaches a wasteland. A stinking smell makes him dizzy; no choice but to search for food to feed himself.

Covering his nose with his t-shirt, he throws empty bottles. An ugly, pink-eyed rat with yellowish sharp teeth bites Alex's right hand! The itchy redness pops in his fingers. Caught an infection! Taking off the t-shirt, he sees a rash on his entire body and screams in pain. It is his fault he came this way for nothing! Continuing west, he walks, feeling sick from this terrible illness, scared of dying. Finds no plants or water!

He sees burned trees and dead plants everywhere. The conditions are worse, with nothing to heal himself. Alex thinks he will not last much longer, hopes someone is on the way to help him. The sun is shining; he spots an abandoned post. Reaching this place, he sees weird stuff inside. No medicine! Searching under the shelves, he sees a vast shadow in front of him. Someone strikes Alex! He wakes up in shock, tied to a wooden fence. He tries many times to free himself.

A strong big man raises his right fist and questions Alex, "Are you stealing my goods?!"

Alex responds, "No, sir, I am sick from a rat bite, looking for medicine. Please help me! I lost my friend, without a home. You are the last who I know to save me. I stole nothing! Search me if you call me a thief!"

He bursts, "Ok, fine! First, I will have to frisk you. You are clean. Let me check on you . . . Don't worry, I will not hurt you. Take off your clothes. Son, you are sick. I can help you recover from your illness, but it will take time."

"I am Alex. What is your name, sir?"

"My name is Arnold," he responds.

Alex questions, "For how long I must stay?"

Arnold answers, "A few days."

He untangles Alex, helps him up, and carries him back to his post, descending to the den where he lays Alex on a splashy bed. Alex falls asleep tucked under a warm, cozy blanket, having close company with someone new. Arnold whispers, "You need to rest."

After having a long sleep, Arnold brings medicine, and Alex thanks him for it. A few days pass and he is ready to continue his journey home. It is a late afternoon and Alex rests while waiting for Arnold to cook food. Takes a short stroll to breathe fresh air after staying four days inside a den.

A half-hour later, Arnold calls Alex, "Dinner is ready!"

On a lunch table beside the house, delicious barbequed hot dogs with fresh sweet corn. Alex is starving and tastes the spicy sausages in a bun.

Alex compliments Arnold, "The food is delicious!"

Alex enjoys eating dinner in good company while hearing the sounds of nature and birds chirping. Full to the stomach after eating four hotdogs, an egg salad sandwich, and three sweet yellow corns! This evening, Alex will speak to Arnold. He goes for another short walk. A great idea. Coming back, he sees Arnold is working.

Alex speaks, "Arnold, I am leaving tomorrow on a road journey. My parents are waiting."

Arnold speaks, "Why? Can you stay with me for longer, keeping me company? I have no one to make friends with since my wife died three years ago." Cries.

Alex responds, "My dearest friend Freddy died. I cannot stay, but you can come with me."

Arnold argues, "No! This is my home! I will not abandon it, risking death! Sorry, Alex, you are strong enough to survive without me!"

Alex is mad at Arnold. "I am leaving! Thank you for your generosity in curing my illness!" Alex storms out, not looking back.

Scared of knowing what might happen, Alex wonders, Is hell breaking loose? He cannot imagine the effects caused by tragic natural disasters. Nothing will stop him from moving forward! He will fight to the last bone, saving his hometown from another catastrophe!

Alex stands on a low hillside before an abundant grassland with animals and great scenery. Everything has changed! Not tired, Alex continues further, strolling towards an extensive set of trees, finding the perfect spot to think. The tree is tall enough to shade him from the sun's ultraviolet radiation; he sits on the moss, thinking of a safer return home. Alex faces a tiresome journey with tough decisions, a nightmare of being a lonely survivor troubled by making false predictions. He is sad with a blank mind.

Alex keeps going till his days are done. Stands up and stretches, giving himself a minute to energize before the long travel! Jogging so as not to waste time, he is off on a road trip! Unafraid. After eating a wholesome meal back at Arnold's place, Alex has plenty of energy to run and kill, and for the spirit to stay alive.

Alex sees the grassy landscape and gains speed, running towards the mainland. Challenged by the hardships of life which he cannot escape. God has given him the choice to either live or die; he must choose between those two.

Trees surround Alex and he's passing through the habitat as an athlete, not losing his pace. No time for resting. Every moment counts as he explores unknown places with caution and follows strange paths.

Tired after two long hours, Alex walks. His shadow disappears when the sun fades behind the dark clouds, and he looks beyond at an approaching thunderstorm! Nowhere to hide. Trapped! Alex sees a wall of heavy rain headed straight his way and the wind gusts, damaging trees! A storm is coming! Caught under the drenching rain.

Huge rain droplets soak Alex and the loud sounds of thunder scare him. Stepping on puddles through blowing rain, hail hits his forehead; in front of him, a lightning bolt strikes twenty metres away! The crashing sound of a catapult deafens Alex. Falls to the ground! It's still raining heavily, and he hears the rumbles of thunder; no choice but to continue this trip.

No one to save Alex from this severe storm. He is in danger and cannot escape. Cannot speak from the panic attack. Alex is soaking in his wet clothes, bare feet in thick mud. His hearing is better and he stands, shaking in fear, afraid of being struck by lightning.

The winds ease and the storm clouds disappear. The fields turn into the depths of a lake! Alex never expected this disaster would happen. He gives himself the chance to continue his journey before it's too late. Soggy weather depresses Alex after the fight with Arnold. Trying hard to achieve a longer life expectancy, Alex is a brave survivor who does not quit.

Alex plunges into the flooded marsh and swims through the hogweed, not touching any poisonous plant. His health is at high risk, the itchy redness on wet skin. With a good pair of eyes, Alex spots a massive rock and sits on it, resting. Thinks of his next moves, nothing comes to mind. Alex comes out from the water and stands in exhaustion.

No clothes to wear. Alex runs for his life in circles towards nowhere. Will he intensify his efforts to become stronger? This is his chance to redeem himself as an intuitive and competent person.

Pushes aside a heavy log, he makes it through the narrow corridor, glances at the hillside, and follows straight towards the large pond by avoiding dangerous shortcuts. Alex takes a deep swallow in fear of losing his breath, forces himself to go on and not play chicken, jumps across the pond, halfway. In front of him, a big viper snake strikes!

Alex does not make any sudden moves. How will he pass through this venomous serpent? Cannot imagine himself being bitten and on the verge of death. No branch or rock for creating a diversion. It is Alex versus the deadliest predator.

The viper snake shows its loud warning in an attack position. Alex takes his clothes off, and throws an old, ripped shirt and, in a blink of an eye, it turns its head away and moves closer and closer! Alex has nothing to defend himself with, no other choice but to escape. The serpent lies in the same spot.

Alex finds a lengthy tree branch—his last chance to kill the viper snake. It awakens after he bends, grabs it, and pulls it with his tired arms. Seeing its eyes open and mouth full of sharp, pointy teeth in a vicious attack, Alex prepares himself, holding the branch high, and the snake snaps! He hits it hard a few times on its belly and it lies on the ground, not moving! He goes around this snake, six metres away from it. Alex has survived the deadliest attack of this journey.

Alex heads towards a desert where dead trees are dried to the last shrub. Runs naked with a terrible sunburn, without water. Tired of running long distances, Alex has low energy, with no power to fight the challenges for brave survival. He is an outcast. Finds no food to feed an empty stomach.

It is turning out to be a scorcher. Alex feels the sweat dripping from his naked body and sees his arms turning red from the blistering sun while walking on sand towards the hottest vortex, no shade. His bare feet burn on the hot sand, with nothing to cover his head. The sunny skies make it too hot to withstand the terrible heat. Tries to stay awake by not fainting. Dizziness won't stop Alex from continuing further! He is a proud, brave survivor and will never abandon a chosen destiny.

Alex heads south to find more survival resources and water, with doubts. Has one choice: to kill an animal to survive the drought. It is going to be hard to spot a roaming creature within the wilderness where anyone who wanders dies.

Not looking for trouble, Alex cannot imagine risking his life for failure, has learned little from his survival lessons. The one survivor left on this planet to fight with no protection. Not taking a step, Alex is dying in the middle of nowhere. Worried about his parents back home, he always dreamed of flying in the wind, seeing the world below on a parachute.

Not expecting the early sunset, he feels the chills in his body. Ahead, Alex sees the radiant sunset where the dark sky appears luminous. He cannot watch the blood sky fill with haze when it turns darker. No place to sleep but lie on the hot desert sand.

Invisible stars, difficulty making a campfire, everywhere is dark, no sounds of animals nor the wind. Danger might happen. Alex does not close his eyes and he stands awake to keep watch for danger. Sits on the rocks naked; he will follow where the sun will rise.

Wondering if this plan will work, Alex must fight to the death. Waiting every moment for the sun to appear, he hopes he will soon find his home in a safe return. Alex closes his eyes. Awakens later, seeing daylight! He stands up in excitement, looking at the sunrise beyond in the distance at a south-eastern angle—his home. Trees are well recognized. Alex guesses, comes closer to the right path. No point in staying. He walks, following the sun on the horizon. Not tired of continuing; Alex has his last chance. Extreme dangers in the outside world are coming. Must pay close attention.

The sun is high and the warm weather suggests it will be another scorcher today, which won't stop Alex from resting again; no time to be playing games. He strolls, searching for food and figuring out which path to avoid dangerous shortcuts within the wilderness. The sun's rays hit directly at his weak eyes, making him dizzy with red vision!

Alex shakes his head twice. "You can do this!"

In the scorching afternoon, steam is coming from the burning ground. His feet turn red as a tomato! Alex cannot tell how many hours he has walked. Reaching the far west, he sees the mainland. Walks with double-vision, sees thousands of deceased bodies across the eroded valley!

No appetite. Alex looks around in shock at the tsunami's aftermath! Paralyzed young children's bodies lie dead in their school uniforms. He finds one with a familiar face. It is Donald McGregor, who was Alex's closest friend from gym class! A superb athlete. They both played basketball together during recess. The town has turned into a bloodbath! Alex is the last person alive to bury dead bodies! Freddy's parents are not alive!

The brave survivor becomes a grave digger with no shovel to bury the dead. Alex strolls through a degraded field where he smells blood vaporizing from the hot surface of bodies. Earth's destructive forces have obliterated the innocent lives of humankind. People won't live to see the end of 2042. Alex counts every body lying in close proximity, estimates fifty thousand lives are buried in the tomb of ruins!

The winds gust, and the fog spreads fast, blankets everywhere. A finger pokes Alex's right shoulder where he stands still. Turning around, he looks back, sees nothing. From nowhere, Alex hears Freddy's loud voice in the wind!

Alex shouts, "Freddy, is it you?!"

Through dissipating mist, Alex sees the ghost of Freddy through a grey sky. Alex runs. The power of Freddy's return from the heavens shakes the ground much worse than an earthquake! The sky spirals, sucking in dead bodies. Alex takes cover, closes his eyes, afraid of dying. He peeks with his left eye, flying high as a bird. Everything is spinning within a deadly vortex and the funnel cloud swallows Alex!

Alex falls through the rain clouds, hitting the terrain, and glances beyond the horizon at a reborn world. Freddy has restored civilization, and he has shown his superhuman power to save Planet Earth from collapse. Alex stands on Earth's wretched ground and watches the dead come back from the afterlife!

CPSIA information can be obtained
at www.ICGtesting.com
Printed in the USA
LVHW041310160523
747083LV00001B/24